The
Neighborhood

By

Charity Pleasant

Disclaimer

"The story does not reflect any real neighborhoods or persons. Any similarities are purely coincidental."

Dedication

First, I'd like to give God credit for all of my accomplishments. Through him, I find all things to be possible. I dedicate this book to my son, who is and always will be the light of my life and my proudest accomplishment. Every time I look at him, it drives me to push myself further than I ever think I can go, if only to brighten his life. Love you, Jordan!

Acknowledgment

I'd like to acknowledge my mother, who is no longer physically here with me, but I still can hear her proud words that she'd inevitably have for me. It was she, I remember, who first put a book in my hands, which began my love of reading. I'd also like to acknowledge Maddy D., who made first-round edits for me, making my manuscript way more polished than I could. I also want to acknowledge the "Grove City Writers' Group" who welcomed me into the fold, encouraged, listened, & and cheered me on during my drafting stages. It's always a pleasure being in the room with so many talented writers who inspire me to dare to dream of seeing my words available to all.

I'd also like to acknowledge my two brothers, two sisters, and my dad, who've supported me from book one, two, three, and are thrilled every time I continue to write. I will always be their biggest fan and cheer them on in life and all their accomplishments.

Table of Contents

Chapter 1

Chelsea

It was moving day! I was so excited that I had found a place to purchase before my landlord slipped my current rental right from under me and my twelve-year-old daughter, Ariel's feet. We had been renting the house for seven years, at least five longer than I had originally planned. My landlord informed me that he had sold the property just before Christmas. The new owner wanted me out so that the rent could be dramatically increased.

I had searched for months to find something to rent or buy before we ended up on our rears. But the market was so volatile; it was terribly expensive to buy, and the rent was at least three times what I was paying. Then, there was the competition. Whenever my realtor took me to see a house, no sooner than we went to put an offer in than the house was sold. Buyers were paying cash, houses were only on the market a day or two before selling, and most were going over the asking price.

So, when I came across this cute, little two-story house with HOA fees under my budget, I had my realtor put in a full-price offer even before we did

1

the walkthrough. I could not have my daughter staying in some low-budget hotel if we couldn't find a place to stay.

So, here we were, backing the U-Haul into the driveway of my first home purchase since my divorce eight years ago. Just as we stepped out of the U-Haul, my two male friends and coworkers pulled up to the curb, intent on helping me unload. Honestly, I don't know what I would have done without them. I had no siblings in town, and I certainly didn't want to ask any of my former in-laws to help. I'd offered to pay my coworkers, but they said they'd take a six-pack as payment.

"Sean, I wasn't driving too slow for you and Arnold, was I?"

"No, we were just seeing how slow we could possibly drive without going to sleep," Arnold said.

"Oh, shut up. I really appreciate you two helping me unload this stuff. My brother, cousin, and uncle helped me load it all, but the three of them had somewhere to get back to. Ready to get started?"

"We're all set."

"Alright, great. Let me sit Ariel in the living room to play on my phone so she'll be out of the way. Be back in a jiffy."

When I returned, the guys already had the U-Haul's door up and gloves on.

"Great, so I have all the boxes labeled with where they need to go, like the kitchen, bathroom, bedroom, and whatnot. It should be pretty straight-forward. If you find something not labeled or sitting in there loose, like that lamp back there, just ask. All the big stuff for you two to haul in is in the back."

"Ten–four," Sean said. Then we all got to work.

I couldn't believe how fast the U-Haul was emptied. It only took about 90 minutes. It felt like it had taken so much longer to get it all packed and loaded. I gave Sean and Arnold their six-packs; little did they know I also stuck an Amazon gift card inside and sent them on their way.

I was standing in the driveway waving goodbye when a man approached, giving me a wave and a smile.

"Hi, you must be our new neighbor, Chelsea," he said, sticking out his hand for me to shake. "I'm Frank, the HOA president. Welcome to the neighborhood."

"Hello, Frank," I replied and returned his handshake. "Nice to meet you."

"I'm not sure if you were aware, but the previous owners, the Whitmans, just relocated out of state for a new job."

"Oh, okay. That's exciting for them."

"Yes. And your neighbors next door to the right, the Walters, usually work all day, so you won't see them much until the evenings. But your neighbors to the left work the second shift, so you'll hear and see them most mornings, but the evenings at their house are quiet. They don't have any children."

"Oh, noted."

"Rhonda's in that house across the street. She lives alone, but you should watch out for her; she's sneaky. So is Mike just next door to her." He gestured at the houses as he spoke. If I didn't cut this conversation short, there was no telling how long he'd keep me standing there. I cut in just as he opened his mouth.

"Well, I don't mean to interrupt, but I have a lot of unpacking to do, so I'd better head back inside. It was lovely to meet you, though."

"Yes, it was lovely. I'll have to catch you up on the neighborhood happenings soon, Chelsea."

"Sounds good, Frank. Have a good day."

"You, too. Oh and let me know if you need any help inside. I've been inside your house so many times when the Whitmans lived there. I know the layout well. Bye."

As I closed and locked the door once I got back inside, I thought about how weird Frank's last comment sounded. I mentally noted all the gossip he'd just told me and turned to check on Ariel. I could process it later.

"Alright dear, it's time to give Mom back her phone." Then I laughed as I checked the time. "It's amazing to me that you sit for ninety minutes without as so much as a peep whenever I let you play on it."

"Aw, Mom!" Ariel whined. "When are you going to get me my own phone?"

"No time soon, that's when." Then I changed the subject. "What do you think of our new home? Isn't it nice?" "I mean, it's fine, I guess. My bedroom is bigger than yours, so I have space for all my board games and puzzles."

"I'm happy you have the bigger one if that's what you want. Mine is still pretty spacious even though it's smaller than yours. Why don't you head upstairs? We'll start unpacking your room first."

"Okay, Mom."

While Ariel walked upstairs, I stood in the living room, taking a moment to congratulate myself for securing a home for us. I slowly turned, looking at the walls, ceilings, and floors, appreciating every detail of our new home. Now the neighborhood, I wasn't so sure about. But what could a little gossip hurt anyway? I never paid too much attention to our last one.

Chapter 2

Frank

As I walked back down the sidewalk to my house, I'd already decided to pull Chelsea's file back up and review it on my computer. As the HOA president, one of the advantages I have is that every new buyer has to submit their personal information to the HOA board for record keeping.

As I was sitting on my porch watching Chelsea and two other men unloading the U-Haul truck, the first thing I noticed was that the two men drove off. So, did that mean she was single? Widowed? Divorced? I saw the child enter the house prior to the unloading and assumed she was Chelsea's. No one even saw me watching as I inventoried all the things that were unloaded. Well, I'd just have to see how she would fit into our neighborhood.

As soon as I walked into my house, I went straight to my computer. I found a file from her realtor with an attachment labeled, HOA REGISTRATION in my email inbox. I clicked on it immediately and started to read. According to the file, Chelsea's daughter was twelve years old, and she and Chelsea were the only two registered as occupants. I was right. She didn't have a significant other. I wondered why not. She was beautiful. I noted other details. The car space said blue GMC SUV; on the job line, it said schoolteacher and no pets were registered.

Everyone said schoolteachers were so under-paid. But I always thought they'd had a pretty good setup with having all the weekends, holidays, and summers off. I clicked the red ex signaling my computer to close out all open boxes, signed off, and shut my computer down. I leaned back in my office chair and thought about what her daughter might look like. If she looked anything remotely like Chelsea, she was indeed beautiful, too. I couldn't wait to introduce myself to her as well.

I wondered when that opportunity would present itself. Of course, I could always be neighborly tomorrow and take over a housewarming gift to try and get a glimpse of her. *Yes. That's exactly what I'll do. But what could I take over that would be appropriate?* I don't cook. If I did, it wouldn't be anything suitable to eat. *Flowers. Yes. I'll take over some flowers tomorrow, that's it.* I was getting excited just from the mere thought of seeing Chelsea again. If I happened to see her daughter, too, that would be a bonus.

Chapter 3

Rhonda

I closed my blinds after I saw the U-Haul truck drive off. The morning had been interesting as I watched my new neighbors across the street unloading their possessions. I secretly hope they'll be more interesting than the Whitmans were. To be quite honest, they were pretty boring. Nothing exciting happened when they lived there. They were just a typical middle-class family of do-gooders. *Blah!*

There are usually conversations to listen to when I have my windows open at any given time of the day. At least, that's something. Then there are times I'm sitting on my porch and watch Frank taping an HOA violation for the wrong color paint or flowers in a yard that don't seem to wilt because they're fake. I mean, who has time to nickel and dime all the tiny code violations, anyway? How would anyone even know that a house had fake flowers unless one was looking way too closely or bending down to touch them? *Who'd care anyway?*

I'd been in the neighborhood for ten years now, longer than Frank. Most of the people who moved here usually stayed for five or six years. A few have lived here just as long as I, like Mary, Patricia, Mike, and Lisa. Most of them had some deep-rooted issues with Frank that I never got twisted into.

Apparently, Mary and Mike, who are siblings, used to be on the HOA board and now they're not. I didn't know what they had against Frank, other than being such a gossip. According to him, it had something to do with the two of them doing something they weren't supposed to when they were on the board. But like I said, I did my best to stay out of it. It's just that Frank wouldn't let me. Once he started talking, he didn't as much as take a breath. So, I couldn't get a word in edgewise.

I had to admit, there was hardly a thing around here that Frank didn't know about. He stuck his nose in everyone's business. *Hah.* Frank didn't get a crumb out of me. I could talk a whole conversation without giving away a single detail about myself. I stayed private when it came to this neighborhood. Don't get me wrong, I was friendly, but no one knew that much about me. I was sure Frank read the two little details on the HOA registration we filled out bi-annually, but that was it; that was all the information Frank got about me.

My two children take turns visiting me after my husband died three years ago. I have lunch occasionally with my old friends sometimes too. I do my own grocery shopping; no need to be lazy like my neighbors who have theirs delivered. Why do that when my feet worked just fine?

I'm not super curious about the new neighbors, so I won't take over a housewarming gift. I don't think it'll matter since Frank most definitely will. He does that sort of thing for everyone who moves into the neighborhood. I figure I'll just wait until I cross their paths while we're both outside at the same time and say hello then. Time would tell what sort of excitement they would bring. Or not. I'm not in any rush to see it.

As it is, I'll just keep doing the things that I always do to keep myself busy. Like sending those anonymous letters to the HOA PO box with all the code violations I've found. It gave Frank something to do. Lord knows his life would be boring without it. I mean, I hadn't seen a woman visit him in the ten years I'd been living here. Why was that? Not that I was looking or anything, but Frank's not horrible to look at. I wondered if Mary or Mike had any insight into Frank's past... Maybe neighborhood gossip isn't so bad after all.

Charity Pleasant

Chapter 4

Patricia

Why am I always the last one to find out about things around here? My husband and I pay our HOA dues on time every month. It's not that I'm not looking forward to having new neighbors. But I didn't mind that Whitman's house sat empty for nearly three months.

I've been living here longer than everyone else, but somehow, I find out about everything last. I mean, it might be my fault. I realize my husband and I are busy with work. He's a top executive at a prominent company. I'm a business owner, but still. We're like the neighborhood patriarchs. Or something like that. Wait! Pillars in the community. Yes, that's it! We're pillars.

Our rise to status happened only because of the hard work we put in early in our lives while all our counterparts were playing around with their time. My husband and I are only in our early forties, yet we're both considering retirement in the next five to ten years. Our joint income brings in almost a million dollars per year. We've been able to invest a good amount of those dollars into our futures.

Sometimes, I wonder why we chose this mid-class neighborhood when we could really afford such a bigger or better home. At other times, I appreciate the feeling of not having to keep up with the Joneses. We use all of the HOA rules to our advantage. The neighborhood always looks pristine. In actuality, this neighborhood is a win-win situation. It's safe enough, nice enough, and busy enough to keep me entertained when I make an effort to stay in touch with the latest goings-on. It's not as if we need more space.

I wonder how these new neighbors will fit in with Rhonda, Mike, Frank, and all the rest. We have the annual block party coming up soon. Maybe I'll meet them then. Now that I think of it, maybe it's better that I don't find out about things in this neighborhood. There's no need to stir the pot when there's no reason to. Nobody ever bothers us, so that must be a good thing. Besides, the last time I stood out front to listen to Frank, he was gossiping for nearly twenty minutes. I don't have time for all that.

Frank was telling me about how Lisa, Mary, and Mike were out to get him kicked off the HOA board. He said that they were mad at him because he made sure everyone paid their dues ever since he became president. Shouldn't everyone be paying anyway? I could hardly believe it when he said he had to put up cameras around his house because someone broke out his windows last month. He swore it had to be Lisa, Mary, and Mike behind the whole thing. Maybe.

The thing is, Frank has a new story about some odd thing being done to him almost every other month. Frank always tells me to be careful or watch out for these three neighbors. But I don't see why when they don't bother me.

Chapter 5

Mike

I knew no sooner than when I saw that U-Haul pull into the Whitman's old house, that I would see that S.O.B. Frank waltzing up the street like he owns the neighborhood. I was sitting at my kitchen table, eating my breakfast a little later than normal because I had the day off, when I saw the truck pull in. I cleaned up the kitchen, did some vacuuming and laundry, and riffled through the newspaper to relax when the new neighbors finished unpacking.

I could tell by the young lady's body language that she didn't really want to hear whatever gossip he was saying. But Frank never was one to see the obvious social cues. She must've been relieved when he finally turned to walk back to his house. I wonder how much about me that he shared with our new neighbor. Everyone knows that Frank is a talker; that's no secret.

Neither Mary, my sister, nor myself can stomach him. We can go on for days trash-talking about him whenever his name comes up. We were the most popular people in the neighborhood until Frank showed up. I guess some people really didn't have any excitement in their lives. That's probably why they stood out in their yards and listened to him blab all day. But Mary and I have actual jobs. We don't have time for his exaggerated stories. I know things around here haven't always been on the up and up, but it's not so bad.

I know Lisa can get a little diabolical at times, but who can blame her after all the ways she's been taken advantage of? You wouldn't believe the stories she's told me about several of her family members stealing money from her. Some have even had the nerve to steal valuables from her house. She never has anyone over to her house anymore because of that. I guess she's been burned too many times.

Then there was that one time I caught her outside of Frank's home. One night, really late, I had gotten out of bed after not being able to sleep. I went downstairs to get something to drink, and I heard a noise from outside. I looked out my window and saw a figure in Frank's driveway. Squinting, I could see Lisa's undeniable features with her dreadlocks sticking out the side of her scarf. I thought to myself, what in the world was she doing? I crept quietly out onto my porch just as she bent down on the side of his car with what appeared to be spray paint.

I ran as quietly as I could towards her, whispering her name. I got to her just as she took off the cap and was about to spray the side of Frank's car.

"Lisa?" She jumped.

"What?!"

"You can't do that. I saw you from my window. What if someone else is looking out their window at this very minute?"

"I'm tired of Frank thinking he is so high and mighty."

"Well, there are other ways to get back at him. This is not it, go home."

Her shoulders shrunk as she put the cap back on what I now see as a red bottle of spray paint. It would've destroyed the panels of Frank's white car. And he loved that car.

"I knew I should've just put a nail in his tires," she grumbled. "I could've gotten that done in no time."

I laughed quietly as I returned to my house, regretting I didn't let Lisa follow through with her plans. It would've been a sight to see the reaction from Frank once he saw what she had done.

Now that I think about it, I would've paid good money to see her handy work. I couldn't wait to tell Mary what conspired that night. I knew she'd give herself an ulcer from laughing so hard.

Charity Pleasant

Chapter 6

Lisa

I found out late the other night on our neighborhood app that we were getting new neighbors. There weren't too many details about how many people would be moving into the Whitman's old house, like if it was a family with a lot of kids. I assumed I would not have to wait long to find out. Gossip spreads fast around here. I cannot see the old Whitman's house from mine because I'm the furthest house from it. But I'd bet everything I own that Frank has already introduced himself.

I've been living in this HOA community for about ten years now. Most of my neighbors are pretty typical. I like not having to worry much about safety, unkept lawns, or holiday decorations kept up too long. The HOA has rules about that sort of thing. I've never been too big on bright colors or holidays; that's why an HOA is perfect for me. I don't mind paying the fees every month to keep within certain standards. Frank will put a note on the door of anyone who doesn't comply.

Frank creeped me out with all of his assumptions, personal questions, and the perverted look in his eyes. There's just something about him that makes my skin boil. Maybe it brings back memories from my childhood when my uncle tried to take advantage of me. There was this look my uncle had where I just knew I was in trouble. Thank goodness my dad had taught both of his girls how to defend ourselves if we needed to. That particular day, I was alone in my uncle's home, which usually never happened since I was there to visit my cousin. I fought him hard, barely getting away with most of my clothes still on.

I've never trusted another man since then. Other than my dad, that is. When I told him what happened, he hurt my uncle in twenty ways that I could hardly even imagine. As I stood and watched, I thought my dad would kill him with all of the torture tactics he was using. But he didn't. I was so intrigued by all the things he was doing that I remembered every detail just in case anyone tried something on me again.

After that day, when Dad was at work, I caught animals like stray cats and dogs to see if I could duplicate the methods that my dad used over the years. Turns out that animals don't have nearly as high of pain tolerance as humans. Most of the animals died pretty quickly. Since I'm not squeamish about blood or anything, I work in the emergency room as a surgical assistant.

I basically mop up a lot of blood, move lights and hand tools to the surgeon, and clean up the mess afterward. It's always funny when we get a newbie in who passes out at the first sight of blood. It happens all the time. But me: my eyes stay glued to the surgeon's every methodical cut, stitch, and movement. The ER is exactly where I belong.

Chapter 7

Mary

I remember this subdivision wasn't even complete when I first bought my house here. Patricia was the first to buy. I can't remember whether Lisa or Rhonda was next, but as soon as I had secured my house, I told Mike, my brother, that he had to buy here as well. This is the perfect location between the boondocks and city limits; it's such a private community, and the property values have been steadily increasing every year. Not that I'd want to sell anytime soon, but if I did, I'd surely make double my money.

Mike and I have always been close. We'd defend each other in grade school, protect each other from our alcoholic father, and have always shared a special bond. It was just the two of us against the world. We had just as hard of a life as anyone else, I'd assume.

We didn't starve or anything, but it wasn't easy for Mom to keep food in the refrigerator with Dad drinking most of his paycheck away. After a while, Mom made Dad give her his paycheck. Then, she would give him an amount to drink for the week. She told him once he used it all, that was it. That was when the fighting between the two of them began. Dad always used all the money he had before the end of the week. But Mom was firm with him, and I admired her strength, especially since he could get pretty mean. Mike and I never saw him hit her, but I was sure nervous that he would one day. As scary as the fights were to hear, Mike and I stayed close, even after we turned eighteen, just in case we had to step in and save Mom. Luckily, that day never came.

We stayed home to go to community college while working part-time jobs to help Mom with the bills. We made sure Mom spoiled herself sometimes, too. It wasn't until Dad drank himself to death, ruining his liver, that Mike and I finally moved out. That's how we both ended up here in this community. It was only about twenty minutes from where Mom lived. Now that she's retired, Mike and I make sure that she's still spoiling herself. We pay for her to go on trips with her new friends, shopping, and whatever else she wants. She's been so much happier since our father passed away—and really, who could blame her?

I love my comfortable home here and my neighbors aren't too shabby either, except for Frank. Mike and I don't like him. I'm not sure if he has a certain creepiness or attribute that reminds me of my father, but I just can't stand him. I remember when Mike told me about Lisa almost spray-painting

Frank's car a while ago. I laughed so hard just visualizing the message she would've left. I couldn't believe Mike stopped her. I wish he hadn't. Wouldn't that be the gossip of the century?

Aside from Frank, I go out of my way to be nice to the others in the HOA. I bring a homemade dish to our yearly cookouts, wave at each passing car when I'm in my yard or on the porch and even listen to the boring things they all have to say. I'm the perfect neighbor. I never get any code violations, which I can't say for everyone else. My grass is always cut by professionals, and it's always before it gets too out of control. I'd give the shirt off my back to anyone who needs it. Except for Frank, I'd rather see him freeze to death.

I wonder what these new neighbors are like. They moved in recently. I didn't have time to read the neighborhood app notification until later. I rarely pay it any attention because it's usually like, "Watch out for frost, it's going to be a cold night," or something stupid like that. I'll give them a couple of weeks to settle in before I bake them a pie to take over. Everyone likes my pies. They're actually Mom's recipes, but I know them by heart. Anytime I take them to our neighborhood cookouts, they are gone in a matter of minutes. I wonder what flavor the new neighbors would like.

Chapter 8

Chelsea

Man, who knew a week could pass by as fast as it did? There are still boxes in every room except the kitchen. Ariel seems to be settling in okay. I'm glad we moved in during the summer months so as not to interrupt her time in school. There aren't many kids in the neighborhood, but Ariel mostly plays puzzles and board games alone. She was never really into dolls like most girls. She could play Uno until the sun went down, though. I inevitably join in and help with puzzles while trying to connect with her. I do enjoy a good puzzle; it can encourage the most interesting conversations. Uno, I could definitely live without; it's the game that never ends.

It will be time for me to go back to work soon. As a Social Studies teacher at a high school, I get two and a half months off during the summer. It usually works great, although I'm not so sure this time around. Since my schedule is not routine right now, all the neighbors have a hundred questions about what I do. Especially Lisa and Rhonda. I mean, they seem nice, but the few times I've seen the two of them, it's rapid-fire with their curiosity. I guess I don't mind too much; I would want to know who I was living close to as well.

Frank has been by at least a dozen times to ask if I need anything. Even though I keep telling him no, he keeps dropping in. It would be kind of sweet if I didn't have suspicions that he's currently dating someone. The signs are all there. The constant text message notification sounds, his car pulling back into his driveway late at night. He seems generally nice to everyone—except for Mike and Lisa. There seems to be some sort of tension going on between them. I never see the three of them wave to each other as they come and go like all the others when I'm sitting on my porch having coffee. But I like Mary, she brought me over a peach pie yesterday. I usually don't eat a stranger's food since I have no idea how clean they are. But she brought it over with it still being warm and smelled delicious. It didn't disappoint; Mary can bake really well.

I'm sure I'll learn more about the others once I finish unpacking, painting a few rooms, and socializing more with the HOA gatherings. As a matter of fact, I just got an email from Frank yesterday mentioning there would be a bonfire of sorts this weekend. Maybe I'll join so that the others can get to know me and Ariel. I hope this neighborhood will feel comfortable for us. So far, it seems like my decision to buy here was a good one. Only time will tell how right or wrong I was about it. But for now, It's all smooth sailing with no hint of a storm in sight.

Charity Pleasant

Chapter 9

Patricia

I waved at Mike as I was passing to pull my car into my garage. He was outside watering his lawn for the third time this week. Even though my husband and I could afford it, we only water ours twice per week, no matter how dry it is. Of course, my husband had already texted me that he would be home late again tonight, probably not until nine. This is starting to reoccur ever since he got a promotion at work. I don't know what on earth he has to prove. He certainly deserves a raise as hard and long as he works. Plus, he brings so much money in for the company by bringing in so many new clients each year. I told him he should start his own firm soon. You know, he works for himself. Maybe if I nag him long enough, he'll finally relent and start building his business during the off-peaks of his current job.

As I turned the car engine off and closed the garage, I thought to myself, *Since I don't need to start dinner right away, why don't I go for a walk? I think I will.* This will be a good time to catch up with what's new around here.

I head into the house and upstairs to change my clothes and put on my purple running shoes. Not

33

that I intend to run or anything like that. I go into the bathroom, grab a makeup remover pad, and start wiping my face. Once I was free from most of my morning makeup, I went downstairs, grabbed my phone, and walked out the front door.

Sure enough, I didn't pass two houses before Mary came onto her porch to say hello. "Hi Patricia, how are you doing tonight?"

"Hi Mary, I'm well. I just decided to take a walk before starting dinner. You know how soon enough it will be too cold for me to be perusing down the street."

"I know right. Speaking of perusing, guess who I keep seeing walking over to the new kids on the block? Frank, of course."

"Oh, really!"

"Yes. I swear I've seen him head over there at least half a dozen times in the past three or four days."

"Wow! Why does he keep bothering them? Can't he let them get settled in?"

"My thoughts exactly. I didn't have a chance to find out their names, but I did wave to the mother the other day."

"Oh, yes. Her name is Chelsea and her daughter is Ariel. I baked them a pie from scratch and walked it up to the house the other day. The mom is nice, and the daughter is adorable. That's another reason I hate to see that rat Frank visiting so often. He'll be poisoning them both about all the nails he keeps swearing Lisa put into his tires."

"What? I didn't hear about that. She didn't, did she?"

"Of course not, Patricia. You can't believe a thing Frank creates in his imagination."

I didn't think so. "What would we do without you?"

"Oh, stop it now."

"Well Mary, I better get on and stretch these old legs of mine before it gets too late. See you later."

"Be careful now. Enjoy your walk."

Bingo. I knew all I had to do was go outdoors to some juicy gossip. I should go for walks more often. Maybe that's the key to staying in touch with every· one around the neighborhood.

Charity Pleasant

Chapter 10

Frank

I'm getting used to seeing Chelsea so often now. I wonder how I'll feel when she goes back to work. I wonder why more people don't become teachers anyway. They have the perfect schedules. Not many can imagine having all weekends and holidays off. Well, I guess *I* could, it would be nice. I consider being HOA president as my main full-time job. Plus, I'm really good at keeping things under control around here. Maybe I should consider going into some type of management position if things don't pan out here. But I don't expect that to happen anytime soon. As long as I keep doing what I'm doing, I'm sure things will continue to be fine.

The funny thing is, I thought I heard a noise during the night a couple of months back coming from my driveway. By the time I rolled out of bed to look out the window, everything seemed to be as it should. I looked up and down the street and saw a light turn off at Lisa's house. That gave me a kind of cold feeling. I wondered what she was up to or if I was just being paranoid. Things had seemed to cool down between her, Mike, Mary, and me. But for some reason, I couldn't quite escape the feeling that something might run amiss soon. But I can't linger on it. I have things to do.

I sat down at my computer with my list next to me and started to Google everyone's name in the neighborhood again to see if anything new popped up. You'd be surprised about the personal information that shows up with a single search. I created a fake Facebook profile so I could view others' pages without being found out. People really should make their accounts private. I saw a picture of Mary on the beach with whom I'd guess would be her friends. Next, I saw Patricia and her husband, apparently at some awards banquet or something. They always clean up the best. They have a sort of 'we've arrived' look in their eyes that demands a certain level of respect. I couldn't find an account on the others in the HOA, so maybe they don't have accounts.

I closed out of the search, opened the HOA newsletter document, and began to type this month's messages. My first order of business was to introduce Chelsea and welcome her and Ariel to the neighborhood. Second, I had to remind everyone about the dates that holiday decorations were allowed to be put up and taken down. Thanksgiving and Christmas would be here before I knew it, and everyone is always so excited about putting stupid inflatables in their yards. I'd never desecrate my yard like that. I like the holidays, but I don't go overboard.

I wonder what kind of gifts Ariel likes. I used to get into giving gifts, but I haven't bought anything since the last family with kids, the Whitmans, left. We do get a lot of trick-or-treaters during Halloween, so I usually load up on candy just to see all the costumes the kids wear each year. Ariel would make a cute princess. Maybe I'll look for a unique doll for her this Christmas. Something that couldn't be found in the stores. Something handmade. Yes. That would be perfect.

Chapter 11

Lisa

With Halloween being next week, I put a ridiculous amount of decorations in my front yard again, just to bother Frank. He hates Halloween decorations especially. But our HOA allows them to be up from now until a week after the holiday. You better believe that I won't be taking them down a single day sooner. I do all this even though I could care less about the day, just because I know how it annoys Frank. I always sit out on my porch to pass out candy—the good kind that kids like. Chocolate bars, sour candies, and gum, too. I don't even care if they get any cavities; that's their problem, not mine.

Things have been going well at the hospital. We haven't lost anybody on the operating table since last year when that shooting victim was rushed in. It was a sad situation, with it being an accidental shooting and all. Some kid got into their parents' closet and found the gun. Apparently, he was just playing with it when his father walked into the room and the gun went off. Got him right in the chest. I wouldn't have been too upset if Frank was the victim. Too bad that wasn't the case.

41

I have always believed that kids playing video games with guns in them have desensitized them and made them too comfortable around weapons. Real life isn't like those games where the player gets back up after getting killed. Parents should take more responsibility for what their kids are exposed to at such a young age. Anyway, the doctor tried really hard that night to repair the damage done to that man, but it was too late.

I know how hard the doctor tries in every case, so I always tell him how well his focus is after every operation. I'm pretty sure the doctor is married. I've seen him wear a ring, although he never discusses his wife. My coworkers and I occasionally go out for a drink after our shifts to let loose a bit. But the doctor never joins us. I've gotten to know the people I work with pretty well but sometimes wonder if the doctor is happy. As hard as he works, I hope that he is. Maybe one day, he will let down his walls a bit and let us all in.

"Lisa?" a nurse called from the doorway.

"Yes?" I looked up from my daydream.

"There's a trauma coming in. They're eight minutes out. The doctor would like for you to scrub in."

"Okay, I'll be right there. Let me wrap up my lunch." It was boring anyway; I should have gotten takeout.

"Alright," said the nurse as she left the break-room.

"Duty calls," I said to myself as I stood up, put my lunch back into my locker, and quickly left the room.

Charity Pleasant

Chapter 12

Rhonda

Thank goodness Beggars Night has finally ended. Although I turn my porch light off every year, it's inevitable that a few kids assume I will be giving out candy like all the other neighbors. I don't. And don't think that it eluded me that Lisa has had all those Halloween decorations in her yard again. I know she pulls that stunt every year just to annoy Frank; I think we all do.

Things have finally calmed down across the street at Chelsea's house. For a while, people were coming and going a lot, I assume, to check out her new home since most came with what looked like a housewarming gift. The two of us have talked a pretty good amount these past few months. She and her daughter are starting to grow on me. She reminds me of my daughter, whom I promised to introduce her to soon, which says a lot since I usually keep my personal life pretty private. I don't know when we will have a chance to chat again since Chelsea is back to working full-time. I only keep a part-time job since I've retired to keep me busy, actively moving, and a little cash flow coming in.

My job as foodbank coordinator isn't a hard one, but it's a combination of sitting at my desk and walking back and forth throughout the center. Sometimes, I'm giving instructions to a new truck driver on how to unload the deliveries. Other times, I'm planning where what foods go to when it's time to make deliveries to pantry locations. It feels like I'm doing some good, especially when I secure dona-tions from a restaurant or grocery store that would otherwise be thrown away as unsold food.

I like my job a lot and have been employed there since I retired. The garden that I oversee on the grounds has inspired me to plant my own garden in my backyard. I've been gardening at home for a few years now and really enjoy it. Albeit it's a rela-tively small garden, I give my kids some of the spoils whenever they come over. They always tell me each time that the veggies from my garden are way better than the grocery store. I'm sure they are since I grow without any chemicals or pesticides. They'd be jeal-ous if they knew I'd planned to take Chelsea over a few things next month. That was the real reason why I told them last we spoke that I might not have as many tomatoes as I usually give them. But I don't care. I've been trying to get them to start their own garden for years. But why would they when they could just eat from mine?

I can't wait for my kids to have some grandchildren for me to spoil. I'd love them to work in the garden with me, learning about how food grows. Both of them are no strangers to dating, but I guess they have nobody worthy enough to bring home to meet me yet. Until then, I'll just keep an eye on things around the neighborhood. I haven't seen anything worthy enough to send Frank on a wild goose chase for fun by an anonymous letter for a while. All is on the mend for now. But as soon as anyone steps out of line, I'll be sure to carry out my usual form of justice.

Charity Pleasant

Chapter 13

Mike

I always look forward to this time of year when October turns into November. I get Thursday and Friday off for Thanksgiving, then Christmas Eve and Christmas Day. Those are at least four days I don't have to request off each year. I'm not so lucky with the other holidays, my boss usually lets a few of us request off by seniority. We all know how that works. The same people always get the same holidays off each year. These are the two months I don't have to be mad about it.

Mary and I have a tradition of going to California with Mom for the weekend to sit out on the beach instead of cooking all of Thanksgiving Day. I mean, I have a lot to be thankful for. No one has noticed that I've been cheating the company out of a few dollars every week for about four years now. It's not that hard to do. When the orders come in at receiving, we're always a product or two short when I verify everything. It's pennies on the dollar from the company we order from, so they just write it off. I resell a slew of products in my basement to small business owners at a fraction of what they'd normally pay. It's a win-win for everyone.

49

As much as I've wanted to tell Mary about it over the years, not even she knows about my scheme. I'm not so bad as some of the others in the neighborhood. I cannot forget the night of the HOA Christmas party at Mary's house about three years ago. Everyone was sitting in her living room drinking punch and playing Pictionary, a game that had to be guessed by team members deciphering what a person was drawing. I happened to look over right as it appeared that Lisa had dropped something in Frank's cup. I could've almost sworn it wasn't true until about twenty minutes later, Frank excused himself to the restroom.

It had to be fifteen minutes before Frank re-emerged, at which point he quickly told everyone he had a bit of an upset stomach and had to go home immediately. I was the only one who noticed Lisa's satisfied look on her face, which solidified what I thought was true. I mean, what other secrets do the people in this neighborhood have? I know I haven't drunk anything at parties ever since and have made sure Mary doesn't either. I usually just bring my own beer and I keep it close to me, that's for sure.

As sweet as Chelsea is, I'm sure she's a complete angel. She's probably never even broken a single law or told a white lie. I wonder what she will be doing for Thanksgiving. Will she go to visit her family? Or will her family come to her in her new house?

Maybe Mary will know. She says Rhonda and Chelsea seem to be bonding more than the others around here. I'll make sure to ask when I call her tonight.

Chapter 14

Chelsea

"Ariel?"

"Yes, Mom?"

"Is your suitcase all packed?"

"Yes, it is."

"You have extra undies, just in case?"

Yes, Mom! You always tell me to pack an extra pair, and we never get stranded anywhere, even to need them!"

I can't help but to correct her. She'll learn soon enough. "Well, dear, you never know; there's a first time for everything. I'm glad we're flying instead of driving to your grandparents' house this time. It will mean we can spend more time with the family."

"Is anyone my age going to be there?"

"All your cousins will be there, so you'll have plenty of play time with them. I'm going to pick the rental car up from the airport, so nobody has to stop their holiday food preparations to retrieve us. Plus, I'd like to go a few places in the city while we're there."

"Okay, Mom, sounds good. I'm taking my suitcase to the car now."

"I'll be right behind you."

I ran down to the basement one last time to check that everything was as it should be before we left. Everything was unplugged except for the deep freezer and the two windows, which were securely locked. I confirmed that all the seeds, dried and jarred foods I had stored inside the dark bottles were untouched. I'd been buying them a little at a time from various places over the years in case of a national emergency like a food shortage. Ariel knew not to touch them unless we were in the middle of an apocalypse.

I had been obsessed with being prepared ever since I dated a conspiracy theorist. We dated a few years after Ariel was born until I concluded he was just a bit too out there for me. At the time, he showed me his stockpile and I was very interested in his theories until they went too far. I do believe he was trying to impress me; little did he know how lasting an impression he actually made. Now, I'm prepared for anything.

I headed back up the stairs to check on the kitchen for the last time. All appliances were unplugged except the fridge. Just as it should be. I grabbed my suitcase, set the alarm, and headed out the door, almost bumping right into Mary on my porch.

"Oh! Hi Mary! Happy Holidays."

"Hi, Chelsea. I didn't mean to frighten you."

"It's okay. I'm just loading the car on the way to the airport. When are you and Mike heading out?"

"Mike is going to pick Mom up in the morning and we fly out about 11 am."

Oh good! I hope the three of you enjoy the beach. I mean, it would be pretty hard not to."

"Oh yeah, we love it, even if it is only three days. We've asked Lisa to keep an eye on our places while we're gone. Have you asked anyone to watch yours?"

"I didn't ask anyone, but Frank volunteered, so I took him up on the offer."

"Sure he did."

We both laughed.

"Well, we have to go if we want to get through checkpoints on time. Bye."

"See you later, Chelsea. Tell Ariel I said Happy Thanksgiving."

"Okay, you tell Mike the same, bye."

I got into the driver's seat, checked that Ariel was all situated, and started off to the airport. Ariel immediately was into her phone so I got to thinking that Mary and I have gotten pretty close over these last few months. So have Rhonda and me. We enjoy each other's company. I mean all the neighbors have been great, but we have seemed to really connect.

They come into my home quite regularly to have a drink in the kitchen or chat in the living room. I also go into Mary's home for the same, but not Rhonda's. There's just something I can't quite put my finger on about Mary. It's like she's *too* perfect. There isn't one thing that jumps out at me as to why I feel that way; I suppose it's just a feeling. Anyway, she's been a good friend, so I'll just leave it at that for now.

I reach over and pat Ariel's leg. "Alright sweetie, let the fun times begin!"

"Yeah, yeah, yeah, Mom, whatever."

Chapter 15

Frank

The thing I'm always thankful for the most this time of year is a quiet Thanksgiving. This year didn't disappoint, with neighbors traveling to and fro to be with family and friends. It's nice just to have a little peace and quiet for a change. Of course, I keep an eye on everybody's house, but as usual, nothing is out of the ordinary.

I never go and see my family, at least the ones I have left. My parents have been dead for several years now, and I'm an only child. I have a few uncles, aunts, and cousins, all of whom I've never been close to because there were no family reunions, birthday celebrations, or any of the like. I guess that's why this neighborhood is so important to me—everyone is kind of like family.

I had a family once, a girlfriend and a daughter. It was serious, too. We'd been together for nearly five years when Kaylee was born. I was the happiest man alive. I adored Kaylee and my girlfriend Molly. I thought we were a happy family until one day, I came home from work to find that Molly had taken Kaylee and left me for another man. The note said she wasn't happy for quite some time. But how did I miss it? I thought we were in love.

I still don't know how she convinced our seven-year-old to go with her. After all these years, it still hurts. I've been looking for Kaylee for nearly eleven years now, and I'll never stop looking for her. I sometimes sit and daydream that she is searching for me somehow. What kind of mother would take her child away from her father? I wish I knew the answer to that.

The funny thing is, Chelsea looks like Kaylee, or at least what I think she'd look like today. That's why I can't seem to stay away from her. She reminds me so much of my daughter. I haven't seen Kaylee for so long, but I have a picture of her I always keep by my bed. Nobody in the neighborhood knows about my daughter, as I've never told anyone. I don't want to hear all the sad things they would say. Neither do I want to see all the looks that I'd get afterward. That's part of the reason I moved here in the first place: to get a fresh start.

My night cleaning job keeps me from thinking too much. It pays well enough for me to have the necessities. Plus, I have a little flexibility if something comes up. I get paid for an eight-hour shift but often finish in six. The HOA keeps me busy enough during the day and leaves a few minutes to squeeze in to do my detective work to find Kaylee. Hiring a PI was too expensive to do. You wouldn't believe the hoops I had to jump through years ago to prove she was even my daughter. Molly had taken her birth certificate.

There have been no leads. It's like they both just disappeared from the face of the earth. I don't think the police are still looking. It's kind of a cold case now. Molly will have to slip up sometimes. It's only a matter of time before she contacts one of her relatives or leaves her fingerprints somewhere. I have to let that get me by one day after another until I find her. Or she finds me.

Chapter 16

Mike

"Mom had the best time this holiday, don't you think, Mary?"

"Yes, Mike. It's so great to see her smiling so much these past few years."

"Do you ever think about Dad?"

"No, not really. Honestly, I'm kind of glad he drank himself to death. If he'd lived for several more years, I think it would've taken a toll on Mom."

"You're right. I know he wasn't father of the year or anything, but I still think of him occasionally."

She changed the subject. "So, have you stopped Lisa from doing anything crazy lately?"

"Ha! Not really, lately. But don't leave your drink unattended around her."

"What do you mean?"

"You never know these days what people might do and why they do them."

"You know something, don't you, Mike?"

"Let's just say my circle of trust is shrinking smaller and smaller. I know we can't stand Frank either, but I don't think the two of us would ever try and poison him."

"What?! Lisa tried to kill Frank?!"

"I don't think she tried to kill him, necessarily. I just saw her slip something into his drink that made him sick. She got a real thrill out of too."

"Why didn't I see the whole thing? You always get front-row seats to all the drama."

"The universe likes me better."

"Oh, shut up. I've got to go. My laundry's done in the dryer."

"Okay Mary, talk to you later."

"Later bro, bye."

I'm glad we were ending our conversation. It was time for me to go make some deliveries. Business has been steady, and I've been really careful with whom I sell to. They had to be all mom-and-pop businesses that make just enough to fly under the radar. I also set a fake invoice using a PO box and a fake business name. When people need refills, they leave me a message on my burner phone so things can't be traced back to me.

I wonder how long I can keep this up. I don't want to press my luck. Frankly, I can't even believe I haven't been caught yet. What will happen if I am caught? I can't see myself going to jail. At worse, the company would probably fire me and make me pay all the money back. Sometimes I mark everything as present on shipping and receiving, just so nobody suspects anything. Maybe I'll start verifying every-thing present more often just to cover myself. Yes. I think I will more often.

After packing the back of my car and shutting the trunk, I opened the garage door to back out. Be-fore I even got out of my driveway, Rhonda was wav-ing me down with a worried look on her face. I rolled down my window.

"Hello, Rhonda."

"Mike, did you hear?"

I shake my head. "Hear what?"

"Patricia's husband got in a car accident."

"Oh no! I didn't hear anything about that. When did this happen?"

"Apparently, just a couple of hours ago. She left the house frantic on her way to the hospital. I hope he's okay. Patricia would be devastated if he's not."

"Oh my gosh, that's just terrible. Okay, well I have to go, thank you for telling me. I hope he's okay."

"Yeah, me too. Me too."

Chapter 17

David

As I opened my eyes and began looking around, I realized I was in a hospital room. With all the stark white, beeping machines and people above me in scrubs working rapidly. I'm trying hard to remember what scenario has brought me to this point. I must've hit my head because it's aching in time with my heart.

"Mr. Walters, can you hear me?"

"Yes," I said barely above a whisper.

"I'm Dr. Holstein. You've been in a car accident. We're doing all we can to assess your injuries. So far, it looks like you're very lucky; nothing seems to be broken."

"I feel fine, just a bit of a headache."

"We will take a few x-rays just to make sure all is well of what we cannot see. If everything turns out as well as I think it will, we'll observe you overnight and release you in the morning."

"Okay, Doctor, thank you." I closed my eyes.

Just then, I see Patricia rush into the room as frantic as ever.

"David? Oh my God! Thank goodness, you look alright. You gave me quite a scare; what happened?"

As I think about the answer to that question, suddenly, the chain of events starts to come back to me. Now, I must think quickly about how I will get my story straight. "Patricia, calm down, I'm fine. The accident wasn't that bad. The doctor says I will be fine, and they will release me tomorrow."

She kisses my forehead lightly and grabs my hand. "I got here as soon as I could. I was so worried. Are you sure that you're okay?"

"Yes. My head hurts a little. I wonder if I hit it on the airbag or the steering wheel."

"Where's your car?"

"I don't know, but I'm going to shut my eyes and get a little rest. I'll worry about everything else later."

"Okay, well, I'm going to talk with your doctor. I'll be back shortly."

Patricia kisses me again and exits the room as I close my eyes.

With her gone, everything floods back into my memory. I had my cell out as I was walking to my car from work. I was reading my secretary's text message about where we would meet this afternoon. She had been flirting with me for quite a while now. I ignored it all at first. But she was persistent. Leaning over my desk in mid-drift tops, brushing up against me purposefully, and telling me all the things she would let me do to her. I kept telling her I was happily married, but she wouldn't back off. Well, I finally caved in.

I realized this car accident may've saved me from cheating on my wife for the first time. I was in the car driving to our agreed location when I clicked on a text from her that said hurry with a picture attached to it as I looked down to open what I guessed would be an inappropriate picture of her— and boom. That's when everything went black.

What was I thinking? How would I ever be able to look my wife in the eye again if I carried this act out? Patricia has been a wonderful wife. How could I betray her like that? Now, I know that I will not. But I was so close to making one of the biggest mistakes of my life. And for what? A few minutes of pleasure. A knock on the head is exactly what I deserved. All of a sudden, feelings of gratefulness and a second chance flood my brain and I know that I will use this opportunity to do the right thing from now forward. The first thing I will do is figure out how to pass my secretary on to another department without drawing too much attention. I know. I will ask around and see if anyone is looking to hire one, then tell them I know of someone who is very good.

I don't think there is a long thread of personal texts to worry about. But I really will get some rest now so that I can figure this all out sooner rather than later. Patricia and I never look at each other's phones. So, I think I'm okay there. I just need to make sure everything turns out smoothly.

Chapter 18

Lisa

"I'm so glad that emergency surgery went well," I say as I wrap my scarf around my locks, ready to end my shift.

"Yeah, me too," my coworker said. "The doctor did an impressive job as usual. So, Lisa, are you meeting us at the bar tonight?"

"No. I have to get my locks touched up while I can get the appointment before Christmas rolls in."

"You're going to miss a good time. You know how we get down." My coworker laughed.

"Yes! I know. But if I don't get into the salon today, it will be months before my loctician can get me in again. But have fun, next time, for sure."

"Okay, be safe out there."

We hug. "You too, and don't do anything I wouldn't do."

Well, that ain't much, she says.

We both laugh while leaving the locker room. My coworker heads left and I head right, running right into the doctor.

"Oh my God! I'm so sorry, Doctor. Are you okay?"

"Yes. I'm fine. Please call me Daimeon.

I should've been more careful coming out of the locker room. I apologize again."

"Don't mention it, I'm completely fine."

"Well, you have a good night then."

"Wait. I have been wanting to tell you, Lisa, that you're the greatest assistant that I've ever had. That's why I request you so often."

"What?"

"Well, when I operate at my best, my assistant just knows when to be silent, when to say something, what tools to pass me, and just overall has the good vibes I thrive on."

"Oh! I didn't know that."

"Yes, so I want to say thank you for all you do."

"All I do? You're the one operating. I'm just an assistant."

"You're more than that. I just want you to know that things go so smoothly because of your talent in what you do. Have a great evening."

"You too, Doctor."

"Call me Daimeon." He laughs.

"Oh yeah, forgot." I laugh, too, as I begin to walk away again, this time much slower so as not to tackle anyone else, feeling quite giddy.

I practically dance to the car and all the way to the hairdresser, feeling high after the interaction with the doctor. I mean, I know he's married and all but man, he sure is fine. Wait. Was he flirting with me? Was I too giddy? Oh, he probably thinks I was a huge nerd! Slow down, Lisa. He gave you a compliment; just enjoy it. Oh, but he said to call him Daimeon. I'm sure I won't call him Daimeon during my shift, though. After all, I'm more professional than that. I will save that for hours when we're on more relaxed time.

I barely remember anything my loctician said during my three-hour appointment. She's known to be a chatterbox. I was on cloud nine, imagination running wild about Daimeon. Or should I say Doctor Daimeon as he appeared in my daydream? I barely flinched when she gave me my total and I passed her my card to swipe. For all I cared, she could've said, $1,000 and I probably wouldn't have noticed. I thanked her as I left the salon feeling sexy and very confident about myself, thanks to bumping into the doctor earlier.

As I pull into my driveway, I see Mary walking down the street. I assume it was for exercise since she's wearing yoga pants, a jacket, and gym shoes.

It's so cold this time of year, I don't understand anyone who exercises outdoors. I waved and she waved
back, but apparently, that wasn't good enough. She
seems to be stopped in front of my driveway, waiting
for me to get out of my car.

"Hi Lisa, how are you?"

"Hello Mary, I'm good. How about you?"

"Well, you know, getting a few extra steps in
before Christmas just in case I overindulge. You
know how it is, all the food and everything."

"Oh yes, I know. The forecast says it will be a
white one, too. That would be just perfect. I love a
white Christmas."

"Have you done all your shopping?"

"Yes," I say, knowing I haven't bought a single
gift. "Got it all out of the way. And you?"

"Oh, you know I only shop for Mike and Mom.
I got that finished eons ago. Well, I better let you get
inside. I'm sure you're longing for a little rest after
your day at the hospital, right?"

"I sure am," I lie because I'm still a bit wound
up. "Well, happy holidays, I'll see you later."

"Bye, Lisa," Mary says as she continues her
walking.

There's nothing I hate more than small talk. I think to myself as I grab all my junk off the car seat and head inside my home. *It's so unnecessary. I know Mary means well, but boy, if I could avoid it I would. Most of my neighbors enjoy the comradery except m*e.

Funny thing is, I haven't thought about Frank much at all these past few days. I wonder now what he is up to. I'm sure he will be handing out his annual Christmas cards soon. He's done that every year since I've lived here. I see him going from door to door, hand-delivering them. It makes me sick. I like the season and all. I just think he does it just to get the attention. Oh well. I'll open and read it, and then it will go into the recycling pile as they do yearly. Okay, it's time to wind down for the evening.

Chapter 19

Mary

As I round the corner again for the last time, I finally start to feel how cold it's getting outside. I didn't notice at first because of how briskly I was moving. That chat with Lisa must've slowed my blood from moving rapidly. I just might have to exercise on my treadmill from here on until the spring. Or at least until we have another sunny day.

As I get back to my house, I hear a horn honking. I looked behind my shoulder as I approached the door and saw Patricia waving and her husband in the passenger seat. I waved back, happy to know that he was okay after the car accident.

I was in a really good mood entering the house as I turned to lock the door and remove my shoes. My phone began ringing just as I was hanging up my coat, I ran to answer. I see that it's Mike.

"Hello, brother, how are you?"

"Cold, that's how I am. How are you?"

"Oh, I'm okay. I just got back inside from my walk. It is getting cold out there, but hey, it is December."

"Yeah. Weather man said we're getting our first snow for sure this week. It will be here in time for Christmas; if it's enough that will stick, Mom will love it."

"Yes, she always loved a white Christmas."

"What did you get her this year, Mike? Let me guess, a weekend trip somewhere." I laugh.

"What? She loves going places with her friends. Besides, she gets way more time off work than I do."

"I know, I know, just teasing. She's just so surprised every year, even though she should be able to guess by now."

"Well, what did you get for her? I won't even bother guessing because you get her something different every year and she just loves it. How are you going to top that yoga gift certificate? She goes twice a week now."

"You'll see, it will be something I know she would use and enjoy. Well, I gotta go get my shower so I can start baking."

"Okay sis, love ya lots. Talk to you later."

"Bye, Mike."

I head upstairs, stripping down as I approach the bathroom. I start the shower and hear my phone ringing again. What did Mike forget? Oh well. Too late now. The bathroom is starting to steam, and the warm water is calling my name. I'll call him back later I say as I step into the heavenly warmth of the running shower overhead.

Chapter 20

Patricia

As I pull into our garage, I feel such gratefulness as I look over at David, my husband, my love, my everything. I grab his hand, just holding it. He stares back at me silently and we just sit for a few seconds. I think we're both realizing that things could've ended up much differently.

"I love you so much, David. I don't know what I'd have done if things ended up with you hurt really badly."

"I love you too, Patricia. You're right; things could've turned out a lot worse. I'm thankful they didn't. Let's go inside."

We both head our separate ways as we normally do after entering the house. Me to my home office. I assume David will want to get straight into the shower. As I open my laptop and pull out my phone to make a few calls, as I suspected, I hear the shower. I know that man way too well, I tell myself.

Just as I finished catching up on all my work stuff, I looked up as David entered the room.

"Hi, love."

"Hi," David says. "Honey, we need to talk."

"Oh," I say. "Come in, honey, sit." I wonder what we need to discuss as he sits quietly. My mind is advancing in so many different directions; after all, the past twenty-four hours have been very eventful.

"Patricia, let me start by saying I love you so much." I listen nervously now. He continues, "I have something to tell you about the accident yesterday."

"Okay."

"Promise me you will let me get everything out before you respond, okay?"

"Okay, go ahead."

"I have this secretary at the office who has been coming onto me for the past several months. She has been all but throwing herself at me to cut straight to the chase. I've repeatedly told her I'm happily married, but she persisted. I made a huge mistake."

My body went completely still as I listened to David talking. I could feel myself holding my breath as he continued.

"Patricia, I was on my way to meet her at a hotel when I got in the accident. I don't know what I was thinking. I regret my actions so badly now because I may've followed through with my plans if it weren't for the accident."

Uncontrollable tears were spilling down my cheeks as I listened to what he was telling me.

"I'm so sorry, Patricia. It isn't that I don't love you. I do. I'm not even unhappy; I'm perfectly happy with what we have. I don't know. In a way I think I was just being a man, you know, thinking I can have it all even though I already do with you. I love you so much. Will you be able to forgive me?"

I grabbed a tissue from my desk to wipe my face as I tried to speak. "You were about to cheat on me? I can't believe you. I thought we were better than that. I appreciate you being honest with me now. But it kind of feels like you've been dishonest with me for the past several months. Why didn't you tell me about her? We could've discussed it. Don't you trust me to be there for you?"

"Of course I do. At the time it felt really awkward, then after a while, it was kind of a nice feeling that someone other than you wanted me. I called the office while I was at the hospital and asked for her to be moved to a different department. It turns out one of the partners was looking for a new secretary. She'll be gone before I return to work."

"That's all well and good, but how do we move forward from here? You broke my trust. I mean, you're telling me you were about to cheat on me. Have sex with another women, and for what? To have your cake and eat it too. I'm going to need some time to process this. I realize your accident was a blessing in disguise, but I still need some time."

"Take all the time you need. I will be in my office catching up on some work. I love you."

"I love you too, David."

And I really do. I love him with all my heart, even though he just fractured it. I lean back in my chair, allowing the tears to flow freely now while thinking of our love. It's supposed to be our love only and he was about to share it with someone else.

Chapter 21

Rhonda

As I'm packing my overnight bag to take to my daughter's house, I hear my doorbell ring. As I approach the door, I can see that it's Frank. No sooner than I opened my door, Frank waltzed right in.

"Merry Christmas, Rhonda. Burr! It's cold outside."

"Yes, come on in, why don't you?" I say sarcastically. Of course, Frank totally misses my jab, as usual. So, I just close the door behind him as he's already taken his shoes off and headed into my kitchen.

"I just love this time of year," Frank says as he hands me a wrapped gift. "This is for you, and I picked it out myself as always. I hope you enjoy it."

"Thank you, Frank," I say as I grab the gift and sit it on the counter. "You want some hot tea?" "Oh yes, please! That'll warm me right up." I begin moving around the kitchen, grabbing herbs, water for the kettle, and two teacups.

"So, what are you doing this year, Frank? Going anywhere special?"

"Not really," he says. "A friend of mine from work has invited me to his home for Christmas Eve lunch. But you know how it is; it feels kind of awkward going to someone else's family gathering this time of year."

Well, you know I don't have any grandchildren yet, so I'm just hanging out with my daughter for a couple of days. We're just catching up on all her shows and movies," I say. Then I realized I've shared more with Frank now than ever before.

"Oh, that'll be nice for the two of you to pig out on your favorite snacks and whatnot.

Your family isn't very large, right?" I ask him.

"Nope. I'm an only child and have been parentless since my folks passed. I'm kind of used to being a loner, though. After a while, I've just gotten used to it.

Sometimes, it's just our plight, Frank. I've gotten used to being alone, too. That's why I enjoy working part-time at the pantry. It keeps me social with people."

You don't seem to socialize much around the neighborhood. Why is that, Rhonda? I've known you for almost ten years, this is the most we've spoken."

"Frankly— I laugh — pun intended. Frankly, Frank, I'm more of a private person. I only let so many people get close to my inner circle. I don't like being a part of foolishness or drama or having to deal with stupid people, to be frank." I laugh again at my choice of words. "I don't mind watching it from the outside looking in, though. But since you mentioned it, I don't know much about you either. Much about anyone in the neighborhood, for that matter. I mean, I hear some basic things here and there sometimes by chatting with people for a few minutes. But I've never felt fully invested. Chelsea has been growing on me lately. She and Ariel don't feel bothersome. I suppose it's because I have children and would love to have grandchildren one day."

The tea kettle whistles, and I go to grab the hot water to pour us both a cup. "Well, spill. Tell me something about you, Frank," I say as I sit across him. I'm surprised by how comfortable I'm feeling.

"I'll tell you something that I haven't told any-one in years," he says. I wait, feeling like I'm really seeing Frank for the first time. As I wait, I see a sort of pain I've never seen in his eyes before. For some reason, my heart aches for him.

"I had a family once—a girlfriend and a daugh-ter." I felt my mouth fall open, but I recovered quickly to not alarm Frank. "We'd been together for nearly five years when Kaylee was born. I was the happiest man alive. I adored Kaylee and my girl-friend. I thought we were a happy family until one day, I came home from work to find that my girl-friend had taken Kaylee and left me for another man."

"Oh my God! Frank, I'm so sorry."

"The note said she wasn't happy for quite some time. But how'd I miss something like that? Was she faking the whole time? I thought we were in love."

"Where is your daughter now, Frank?"

"I don't know," he says. "I've been looking for her all these years." I see a tear roll down Franks' cheek. My eyes are watering, too. I get up, grab some napkins out of the drawer, and pass one to Frank. We both dab at our faces as I double back to my cab-inets, grab a bottle and pour something stronger into our teas. Without missing a beat, Frank continues. "Kaylee was seven years old the last time I saw her. Her eighteenth birthday is coming up soon."

"Frank," I say, "what can I do? That sick witch, how could she?"

Frank stares at me, takes another sip of his tea, then says, "You surprise me, Rhonda." I totally didn't expect that response.

"What? Did you think I would look at you with sad puppy eyes, exclaiming how sorry I was? Well, that wouldn't help."

To my surprise, Frank laughs. To lighten things up a bit, I drop a bomb. "Want to know something else, Frank?" I take a sip of my now twisted tea as he nods his head. "I'm the person who's been sending you the anonymous violations."

With that, we both laugh so hard that we're practically falling out of our chairs.

Chapter 22

Frank

The next morning, I realized if it hadn't been for Rhonda telling me she was packing to go to her daughter's house, we may've sat and talked for half the night. Heck, I've never even been inside her home before. I'm not sure if any of the neighbors have. I don't know what overcame me as I just pushed through her door. It must've been the cold, I guess. But we chatted for hours so organically. It felt like we were long-lost friends.

I only knew a minimum number of details about her from her HOA paperwork, which hasn't changed in nearly ten years. Now, I know she's more of a well-rounded person than I originally thought she was. To think she's been the one leaving anonymous notes all these years. I wouldn't have guessed it. I always assumed it was Lisa; it seems like she hates everyone. Then again, maybe I should give people a little more credit. Rhonda turned out to be quite a hoot.

Now that I think about it, delivering Chelsea and Ariel's gift is what must've propelled me to share my personal story with Rhonda. Seeing the two of them always reminds me of my daughter. For years, I've hand-delivered a simple and thoughtful gift to all of the neighbors at Christmas. It's just something I've done, considering I really don't have any other family nearby. Next year, I will have to make Chelsea's home my last drop-off. That way I won't get all sentimental with any of the other neighbors. Although I'm glad I did with Rhonda, we're going to be great friends.

She convinced me to stop over at my co-worker's home for their holiday lunch. I laugh as I drive, following Google Maps directions. When I arrived at my destination, I knocked and was invited inside. It's not as formal as I was expecting. I enjoy the revolving door type of setup where people could drop in and out, not feeling like you have to be seated at a table. Food stations were set up in every room downstairs so people could brush in and out. The mingling was natural as you bumped into different people throughout. It didn't feel like I had to sneak out when I was ready to go because of how everything was set up— which was perfect for me.

Admittedly after having a great time, I thanked my co-worker and host as I departed. On the drive home I decide I will sit at my computer for the next few days, trying as always to find Kaylee, as I do in every spare moment I have. I'm still holding out hope that it won't be much longer before I find her. At least, I pray that I can find her. Those are the only two things I have left: hope and prayer that God will soon answer me and bring my daughter back to me.

Chapter 23

Chelsea

I'm so glad the holiday season went smoothly and it's comfortably behind me. I mean, I love the season and all, but the stress of all the planning, going, and coming can feel a bit overwhelming. Ariel and I had a good time connecting with all the family and now we have been back at school and work for several weeks. I love this time of the year because it seems to progress at warped speed. Before I know it, I'll look up and it will be spring break. Then, final exams, final grades, and boom: summer break.

I am beginning to see that I love my schedule more than I love the actual teaching. I do love kids, coworker comradery and everything that comes with it, too. But sometimes, it just doesn't feel like the same love I felt when I first began teaching. The curriculum has not improved, in my opinion, the education system as a whole has seemed to turn into a sort of agenda or propaganda. So much so that I'm seriously considering taking Ariel out of public school and enrolling her in a private one. Strange enough, I mentioned this to Frank the other day when he, of course, stopped by uninvited, but his response and recommendations were quite helpful.

Frank also filled me in on Patricia's situation with her husband's accident and I have made a mental note to walk by and say hello to check in with them. I know I haven't been in the neighborhood for long, but I'm starting to appreciate the close-knit community it is. I have to admit, it was a bit off-putting at first, but surprisingly, I'm quite enjoying the closeness.

The warning bell rings, letting me know I have four minutes before I will have to be standing in front of my classroom to teach my last class of the day. So, I snap out of my daydream from my spot in the teachers' lounge and pop up to head back to my classroom. Along the way, I tell a few kids to stop cursing and a few others to stop horsing around and give a few high-fives before stepping into my room.

I opened my laptop, displayed my lesson plans on the whiteboard, and passed out assignments just as the bell rang.

"Good afternoon, everyone!" I began, just as I have all year. "Today's riddle is worth five extra points, so whoever guesses it first will have a significant bump in their grade," I say. I found that beginning my class with a riddle, especially in the afternoon, keeps the kids engaged and alert, at least for a few minutes.

"Alright, listen up. Here's your first clue. It shows three colors…" Hands start popping up. "Second clue: it's all over the United States." Hands raise again as students call out their answers. I ignore them. "The third clue, it gives directions." Hah! The kids seem stumped, and I begin to laugh. "Alright, alright, here is the last clue; Some people run it."

"Oh! I know, pick me, pick me," I heard students saying as I perused the room.

Chapter 24

Patricia

A few weeks had passed since David told me he almost cheated on me. The both of us have been going to and from work as usual. We've been talking during dinner and having surface-level only conversations. But we really haven't addressed the root cause of his almost infidelity. In a way, I wasn't really ready to because I was too hurt. Now that some time has passed, I'm ready to face the music.

So, I take a deep breath as I lock the door to my business this evening, get into my car, and put some relaxing music on for the drive home. All the way home, I'm taking inventory of all the ways I might've played a part in this. Have I been very affectionate lately? Have I given him many compliments? Have I really appreciated him? When was the last time we were intimate?

As I wait at the red light, I realize I may be putting a little too much pressure on myself. We are a unit, after all. Although it takes two to actively and successfully stay in love with one another, I have not been underappreciating him. Of course, I could always make him feel more desired, but what I really want to get to the bottom of is what the two of us feel like we're lacking. Or what can be improved. I mean, on paper, we have it all. Nice cars, nice careers, a nice home, and I feel we're really happy. Or at least sufficiently so.

I can't remember the last time I have been thrilled, turned on, or desired, but I know he loves me. I wonder if he feels the same way. I must've been thinking too long because the car behind me lays on its horn, pulling me out of my deep thoughts. I finally pull away from the light. By the time I round the corner to our home, I've already made up my mind to forgive David. He is the only one for me. I've felt that from the moment we first met. We will certainly get through this mess and get back on track to being in tune with one another.

"For better or worse, right?" I say as I pull into our driveway.

To my surprise, David's car is already parked. The repair shop must've gotten all the work done a little earlier than expected. I thought I would see the rental, if anything, considering I usually make it home before him. I take one more deep breath as I turn off the engine, grab my things, and head into the house.

I first noticed the smell of my favorite cinnamon candle; it greets me as I open the door. I also hear smooth jazz playing over the music system we installed but rarely ever use. I put all my things down in the foyer and walked around to the kitchen to see David setting the dining room table. He stopped and looked at me with a lustful grin. At that moment, I realized that no matter how our conversation started or ended, I knew we would be okay.

Chapter 25

David

After fixing my tie in the mirror this morning, I stared back at the reflection for a long while. I saw all the imperfections, dishonesty, and, most importantly, the pain I'd caused my wife. For the last several weeks, we have just been existing, but far from the connection we used to enjoy. I know that it is all my fault for breaking her trust. At this very moment, I promise to do all I can to gain it back from her because I love her deeply. I want to see her happy and thriving.

My mind goes to work on how I can begin this as I walk down the stairs into the kitchen for my morning coffee. The same scene plays that has been lately; I just catch Patricia in time to tell her I love her before she leaves out of the door for work. I know she's been leaving a little earlier than normal to avoid facing me.

Tonight, after work, we will settle this, I promise myself.

I don't stay as late as I usually do at work this afternoon. Turning off my computer, I left my laptop at my desk instead of taking it home to work more.

101

A few people are surprised to see me packing up early as I gather my things.

"David? You got a hot date or something to-night?" one person asks.

"Yes, as a matter of fact, I do. With my wife." There are a few laughs and hoots as I walk toward the elevator with my plans in tow.

After I get to my car, I pull out my cell to order in from Patricia's' favorite take-out spot, then head off to retrieve the meal. I'm glad I arrived home early because I've beaten her here. I will have time to take a quick shower and apply the aftershave and cologne she likes. Next, I rush around the house, lighting her favorite candles, put some mood music on, and then wonder when's the last time I've done this. It's been a while.

I hear Patricia pull into the driveway just as I begin to set the table. I give her my best sexist smile as she enters the room.

"Hello dear," I say. "Drop your things, wash your hands, and have a seat. I'll take care of every-thing else." She complies and I am grateful. I serve her the food and wine I have put together for us, then assemble my plate and sit. *Now is the time,* I hear my conscience say.

"Patricia?" I begin. "I'm so sorry that I hurt you. My actions have put a rift in our relationship that I would like to mend. I should've told you about the temptation I was experiencing at work. I know now that telling you would've made all the difference in my actions. It's not so much that I wanted her but that she was dangling it in front of me and all I had to do was accept. It felt sort of like a freebie or too-good-to-be-true type of situation. That's the best way I can explain it, like some item on sale that I couldn't pass up. But anything that could destroy what we have, I realize now, isn't worth having. You are the most valuable person in my life, and I will think of you in every decision I make from here on out be-cause I don't want to lose the most important person in my life. I love you and I'm sorry."

She hasn't taken her eyes off me; even when the tears started rolling down her face. For that, I certainly feel guilty. I await her reply as I take an-other bite of food. She finally dabs at her face and then begins to speak.

"David, I love you too. I can forgive you so we can move forward. In a way, I'm thankful for your accident because we wouldn't have known that we needed to reconnect with one another. I didn't real-ize how disconnected we were until these last few weeks. But I promised, I would love you through thick and thin, better or for worse. Things certainly could've gone worse, but thank goodness they didn't. Promise me that you will tell me everything from here on out. We will get back to talking to each other the intimate way we love to do. I want to be included in everything that involves you. I want to be able to root you on or tell you when you need to bow out. I respect your talents and your abilities, and I will always support you and have your back, no matter what temptation you face. Just talk to me."

I can't help myself anymore. I leap from my chair to take Patricia in my arms. I can't believe that love like this exists. I love this woman more than life. I grab her hand, pull her out of her chair, and lead her up the stairs so that my actions will speak louder than words.

Chapter 26

Kaylee

Today is much too beautiful of a day, I think as I stand there on the lush, green grass, barely hearing the minister's eulogy. My mom passed away a few days ago; the doctors say it was from a condition that weakened her heart. Apparently, she knew about this condition for quite a while and didn't tell anyone—not even her long-time boyfriend.

I can't stop myself from crying as I stare at the beautiful coffin that he has picked out for her. Roy has been the father figure in my life for so many years I barely remember my own father. I was around six or seven years old when my mom took me and ran off with Roy to this beautiful, always sunny place in St. Thomas. The only thing I've heard over the years is the story Roy can never seem to stop telling. He hit the jackpot, bought three one-way tickets, bought a cute little house on the beach, and has never looked back.

In the beginning, I asked Mom questions about Dad quite often. But it was hard not to be taken by such a beautiful place like this island. Over the years, as I got more friends at school and every day felt like a vacation, my questions became fewer and fewer. I don't know why Mom wouldn't talk to me about my dad. I had no idea if he cared I was gone, missed me, or whether he even wanted me at all. Mom refused to tell me anything, so I stopped asking questions after a while.

When I was fifteen, Mom and Roy took a boat to a private spot for the day. I used that time to go through all of her and Roy's belongings I could find, searching for any clues about my real dad. The only thing I came up with is a photo of my dad and me. I looked like I was about two or three years old in it. There was *Frank and Kaylee* written on the back. That was all I had of my dad, and I am terrified that his name is the only thing I will ever have.

I was forced out of my thoughts by someone putting their hands on my shoulder.

"Kaylee, it's time to go." I looked up. It was Roy. I hadn't even noticed that almost everyone else had gone already. The two of us were the only ones still there. I looked back one last time through my blurry tears as Roy led me back to our car with his red-brimmed eyes. He must've been crying all morning, by the looks of him. I knew he was crazy about my mom.

I got in the car, put my seatbelt on, and Roy drove off. I couldn't help myself any longer.

"Roy," I said, "why haven't you told me any-thing about my real father all these years?" There was a long pause.

Then he said, "For one, Kaylee, I don't know much about him. Your mom rarely said a word about him, and I didn't ask. I loved your mother from the time I first laid eyes on her. I didn't know at first that she had a boyfriend, but then again, I don't know if that would've even mattered. We had a few conversations. They were all-electric, I mean super-charged. From those moments on, the rest of the world didn't matter to me. Then, I won all that money and told her about it. She told me she had a child, you. I told her to bring you with her and we would run away together, and the rest was history."

"Well, I'm almost eighteen now and about to graduate high school. I want to find my real father." There was a long pause. "Now that Mom's gone, you're the only one that can help me." Roy was still silent. "Well, will you? Help me?"

"Kaylee, I don't even know his last name. I only know his name is Frank; I assume he's from Ohio because that's where I met your mom. I'm sorry, I can't give you any more information than that. When we first arrived here, your mom told me that we lost your birth certificate at the airport, so we got another one, which I signed."

107

I couldn't cry anymore, so I laid my head back on the headrest to take all this information in. I'll graduate in a few months. I could start my search after that. I had money saved from my part-time job so I could fly to Ohio soon to begin to search for my dad. I had missed him for so long that I'd forgotten I'd missed him at all. My memories of him were so vague that I could barely remember the feeling of him hugging me. I got such good feelings when I thought of the possibility of seeing him again. My mom's death brought these old feelings back up again that I hadn't felt in years. I would start my plans as soon as we pulled back up to the house. Roy would have to help me; that's the least he could do.

Chapter 27

Mike

Thank goodness the weather has finally begun to break. Slushing around in the snow with all these products has been a headache. Now that it's consistently above freezing throughout the day, it's been easier for me to deliver products. Who knew the forties and fifties could feel so good? My next stop will be my last delivery—not for the day, but indefinitely. I've been telling all my clients for weeks now that I'm going out of business and sticking with what I said. There's only so long one can get away with "products falling off a truck" or "damaged pieces in a shipment."

I decided that I could no longer risk getting caught at my job for skimming products. In the last couple of months, there have been a few pointed questions along with closer monitoring of shipments. I don't want to risk it; I'm out while the going is good. Heck, I've had a good run. A really good run. I'm not a millionaire, but I've certainly put away more than a few dollars. Not enough to retire or anything, but I don't want to get caught.

I hear my phone ringing as I get back into my car. As I guessed, it's Mary, my favorite girl.

"Hello sis, how are—"

She interrupts me, "You'll never guess what Lisa did this time?!"

"Whoa! What in the world is going on," I say. Mary sounds hysterical.

"Lisa put a sign in front of Frank's house that says, 'A pervert lives here!' Can you believe it?"

"She did what?" I say. "No way, I don't believe it." I hear laughter roaring through the phone. Apparently, Mary finds this hilarious. I can't help but laugh at the thought. "How do you know it was her?"

"Who else would've done it?" Mary says. "I always thought she had a bit of a screw loose, but then you told me about that incident at the holiday party. It had to be her."

"Well, be extra cautious around her; don't get on her bad side," I say, laughing."

"Nobody's worried about crazy Lisa unless your name is Frank." We both burst out laughing again.

"Well, what did Frank do?" I ask.

"You know Frank, he lost his marbles. I was out there yelling up and down the street like a mad fool. I saw him go right up to Lisa's front door; you know,

I had to crane my neck to get a good view. She never opened the door, though I know she was home."

"It must've been a sight," I say. "How's everything else going, Mary?"

"Nothing new here. Just work, checking on Mom, and go home. What about you?"

Same old, same old, nothing new to report," I say. More like I barely escaped getting fired from my job and maybe even a little added jail time for my small-time crimes. "I'm about to grab some takeout and head back to the house. So, I'll catch up with you a little later, okay?

"Alright, bro. Later then."

As I pulled away from the business, I thanked my lucky stars. I'd made my very last delivery. I had one last stop before takeout, though. I was headed to the shredding center with all the invoices and receipts I'd ever filled out. I had to get rid of all the evidence I had of even existing as a business. Of course, some of the business owners will probably hold on to their receipts, but I can't see why they would ever need to contact me. There were never any issues with the products I had sold them. How could they contact me at the fake address and burner phone I used all this time? As they say, "We'll cross that bridge if we get there."

Chapter 28

Lisa

That little gremlin must think I'm stupid if he thinks I'm about to answer the door. He's been banging on my door for five full minutes now. The nerve of the little spawn. I turned my music on and blasted it throughout the house, intent on Frank getting the message that I was ignoring him. I don't know why he thinks I put that sign in his yard. Besides, I've been so busy at work lately, that I haven't had time to expend any energy on him. You know what they say, "An idle mind is the devil's workshop." Why would he think that anyway? I mean, I know I take things a bit far at times, but *come on*. I guess I'm not his only nemesis. I laugh at the thought of Frank having several of them.

I got caught up in the song that was playing and found myself dancing around the house as I tidied up. By the time I finished, I had not heard any noise from my front porch. Frank must've given up and went back to his house. Well, good riddance. I turned my music down and settled into the kitchen to prepare my dinner. It would be baked salmon, the rice I cooked earlier this week, and I'll have to throw in a vegetable with it, too. I always like to have a small portion of meat, a larger portion of vegetables, and an additional side to tie a decent meal together.

After everything was ready, I sat at the dinette, set to eat. Some nights, I sit in front of the television, but I felt like being proper today. Even though I eat alone most nights, I like to use my dining table. It's only a two-seater, but I love the cherry wood; it's beautiful and makes me feel good. When I feel like relaxing my brain and really decompressing, I sit in front of the television with my dinner. On other nights, I might meet friends or coworkers, but not too often. I still feel as though I can only get so close to people.

As I finish my dinner, I think about how well things are going at work. Daimeon still requests me to scrub in on the days that we're both in rotation. We haven't gotten to know one another any better from just the surface conversations at work. So, I just hope his wife's treating him right. He seems like such a great man. If I wasn't a better woman, I might try and steal him away from her. Nah, I'm not the type to do that, but boy is it tempting to try. On that note, I scrape my plate and head into the living room. I flip through a few streaming stations and land on Love is Blind. I guess this will have to do for now. I click play and lean back into the couch.

Chapter 29

Mary

I was sitting on my front porch the other after-noon when I saw Frank storming up the street. Boy! Did he look mad, and I knew exactly why. I put a sign in his yard the other night as swiftly as I could muster and quietly as possible to not wake anyone. He's so predictable; I knew he would blame Lisa. I was counting on it. Sure enough, he banged so loudly on her front door; I'm sure the knocking was heard two streets over. I laughed so hard that I almost burst my spleen.

I'm just having a little fun; it gets a little boring around here if someone doesn't create a little drama. We all know that Lisa has a bad reputation around here because of all the little tricks she plays all year. But no one would suspect me: sweet, quiet, and ded-icated little Mary. I laugh again, just remembering how things went down. I don't think anyone has cameras in the neighborhood since we all look out for each other. Plus, someone from the block is pretty much home around the clock.

Buzzz. The timer wakes me out of my haze, and I head to the kitchen to retrieve the pies from the oven I began making this morning. It's almost

115

Easter, and I love baking a variety of desserts for this light-hearted, no-pressure holiday. Mike and I usually go to brunch at Mom's and mingle with her friends for a couple of hours. It gives her a chance to gush and brag about the two of us to her friends.

I lean closer to sniff the homemade blueberry, strawberry, and apple pies I've made; they smell heavenly. I sat all three of them on the counter to cool, which will give me plenty of time to shower and dress for this afternoon. As I head up the stairs, I make a mental note of my closet. I love wearing a spring dress with colorful placed flowers throughout. Although Easter can sometimes be hot, cold or cool, this year, it's not raining or snowing, but I'll make sure to grab a light jacket as well.

A short time passed when I heard the front door open just as I was about to descend the stairs. I already know it's Mike; he's the only one with a key to my house in an emergency. I had talked to him earlier when we decided to meet at my house and drive over to Mom's. As much as I love my mom, I would never give her a key. She would pop over three times a day. I was actually planning to get Mike to help me load the three pies into my car as well.

"Hey Mike!" I say. "Perfect timing, I'm all set."

"Well, that's a first," he says. "I'm used to wait-ing at least fifteen minutes for you. He laughs.

116

"Will you grab my pies in the to-go containers and put them in the back seat?"

"Sure."

"Thanks. I just need to grab a jacket from the closet. By the way, you look snazzy in your khakis and button-down. I like it. It's not too much, just fancy enough, but doesn't need a tie or anything."

"That's what I was going for," he says as he exits with a pie in each hand.

"Don't drop them!" I yell after him.

He returned to the kitchen for the last one. "No, I wouldn't do that, Mary. Then I wouldn't be able to eat them!" We both laughed as I locked the door and off we went.

Chapter 30

Rhonda

This is the best time of year, hands down because it's finally staying warm enough for me to start planting in my garden again. This year, I went a little overboard buying peas, carrots, tomatoes, bell peppers, cucumbers, and a few herbs. I'm going to have a small farmer's market if I'm not careful. But hey, I'll have a reason to invite my kids over once everything is ready to be harvested.

When I talked to Frank a few days ago, I invited him over to help plant my bounty. We've been talking about once per week since that first long encounter. So, I'm looking forward to seeing him in a few minutes. I start taking all the supplies out of the back door when I hear his voice approaching the backyard.

"Hello! Hello! Guess who?"

"Come on back, Frank," I say. I peered around the corner to see him carrying a water bottle and a pair of gardening gloves. "How's it going today?"

"Oh! Not too shabby, Rhonda, not at all."

"Good, help me bring the rest of the items out of the kitchen."

Frank follows me back into the house and immediately yells, "Good grief, woman! Do you plan to grow food for the entire neighborhood?!"

We both laugh.

"I admit, I might've gone a little overboard this year."

"I'd say," Frank says.

"Well, we might as well get started. I'll grab these heavier bags of soil. You can grab the plants."

We moved in and out of the house several times before finally bringing out all the supplies.

We need a water break and haven't even started planting yet. We both sit down on my lawn chairs and take a sip.

"So," I say, "what's new around the neighborhood, Frank?"

"Well, you've probably heard about the Walters' car accident. Well, David obviously got his car repaired if you haven't seen it."

"I thought I'd been seeing an unfamiliar vehicle pull into their driveway, so it was a rental then?"

"Yep, and it was a nice one too, real nice."

Yep, the Walters do everything in style."

"I still haven't found out any more information about the sign in my yard. Although, my gut tells me it was Lisa. I was so mad at her that I marched right up to her door and banged on it like my life depended on it. She never came to the door and admitted it, but who else could it have been?"

"Yes. She is quite a weird one. Well, let's get started so we can finish before too long."

I directed Frank to this task and that one; I was surprised at how well we worked as a team. I used the same area in my yard as I did the year previously, except I rotated where I placed everything, trying not to deplete the nutrients in the soil. We chatted lightly about this subject and that, all the while laughing at our own banter.

We were close to the finish line when I asked, "Any news on Kaylee?"

"Not really. Every time I think I might be on to something, it turns out to be a different Kaylee. I don't know where in the world she was taken to. For all I know, she could be in another country."

"Well, don't give up, Frank. You will find her soon. The universe cannot be that unkind. She might even be looking for you."

"I sometimes daydream that she is, you know. I just fantasize that my daughter is trying to find me somewhere. I keep a social media page for her, hoping and wishing that one day we'll come across each other. I pray that the day will be soon."

We both pause and look around at the work we've just completed.

"Looks pretty good for two wanna-be gardener connoisseurs," Frank says.

"Yes, Frank, agreed."

"You might be on to something after all. I thought I was doing something with my flower garden, but this serves more of a purpose. I plant every year for aesthetics. I can certainly bring a few flowers to sit on the table and look at, but I can't eat them. I'll have to plan a food garden too, maybe next year, though."

"You should. They're very enriching. And, thanks for all your help, Frank. I normally take two to three days to get all this in. I will be sure to harvest some of our spoils and bring them to you when the time comes."

Frank smiles at that.

"And," I add, "you're welcome to come by and visit your investments anytime you want." We both laugh.

"Are you trying to schedule another visit with me?"

"I just might be," I say, smiling.

Chapter 31

Chelsea

"See you Monday," I say to my coworker as I head to my car after work to head home. Ariel will be home already, and she should have started her homework. Thank God it's Friday! The perk I love most about being a teacher is that we always have a weekend. We very much need the two days in a row to recover from the hundreds of personalities we encounter each day. When the vast cultures are considered, along with each of the student's learned behaviors, upbringings, and ever-changing emotions, a three-day weekend would be more like it.

I turn on some relaxing piano music from my Spotify playlist, then pull out of the lot. These days, I drive to our house almost without thinking. The neighborhood has proved to be a great place both for me and Ariel. Although no other kids are on our street, she has met a few on the next street.

I'm growing closer to the neighbors every day, and even Frank has become that person you just get used to dropping in so often once you just accept it. We all seem to catch up a couple of times a year during an event at a neighbor's house or a block party of sorts. I still wonder who put that weird sign in

Frank's yard a few months ago. I hope it was someone who isn't from the neighborhood. But then
again, that might be worse: a stranger coming
around with no one having an idea of who they are.
Frank told me it was Lisa. I mean, she does seem a
bit out there, but I don't know. Now, Mary, I've always said there's something about her I can't quite
figure out. Could she have done that? I lose my train
of thought as a couple of firetrucks come into view
from behind me. So, I pull over to the right median
as they zip past.

As I get closer to the turn onto my street, my
heartbeat increases as I see smoke in the distance.
A police car is ahead, blocking the street where I
usually turn. Oh God! Ariel. As I approach, I see a
house on fire in my neighborhood, but I cannot drive
any closer because of the cop car blocking entry. As
I turn my flashers on and jump out of my car, running down the sidewalk, I see Frank's house on fire.
Oh God! Lisa has burned down his house.

The officer on the sidewalk stops me as I try
and pass him by.

"Wait, miss, you can't go through. The firemen
are trying to get the blaze under control. It's too dangerous."

"My daughter is home, just two doors down
from the flames," I say.

"Officers have already told everyone to stay inside their homes for safety. Can you call her from a cellphone to check on her?"

I had just thought of that, then quickly turned on my feet and ran back to my car. Three missed calls from Ariel. I dial her back quickly. She answers on the first ring.

"Mom? Mr. Frank's house is on fire!"

"I know, sweetheart. Are you okay?"

"Yes, Mom. I'm fine. There was a policeman using his car speaker to tell everyone to stay inside. I've been watching it all from out of the window. Aside from on television, I've never seen so much water sprayed into a house before."

"Just make sure you stay away from any potential danger. If you start to see falling debris, go into the basement. As soon as it's safe to drive down the street, I'll be home."

"Okay, Mom. I got it." We both hang up. I lean back onto my headrest. Poor Frank, he will be devastated. Oh God! I hope he wasn't inside. He works the second shift. I didn't think to ask the officer if they found anyone inside. My heart pounds again as I race out of my car and back down the sidewalk.

Chapter 32

The Walters

"So, how is your car running since the repair?" I ask from the passenger seat to David.

"It's more comfortable than before, so it rides quite smoothly. The dealership called to let me know a few other maintenance items were due that must've done the trick. So, I like it very well," David says.

"Good. I'm glad you suggested we ride to work together this morning. It was nice spending the extra time with you this morning. Plus, I like that we unpacked our days before arriving home. That means we won't need to talk about work and can focus on us as well as relaxing."

"That's true," David says. "Maybe we can try and schedule this ride share once per week. What do you think?"

"Sounds good to me. I think I can definitely do that."

He takes my hand and kisses it. "I love you, Patricia."

"I love you too, David. But what are we doing for dinner?" We laugh. "I guess we could cook those steaks in the fridge and add a nice salad to go with it. Or we can save them for tomorrow and order our favorite takeout. Hmmm—What on earth?!" I say as we approach our street.

"Look at all that smoke. Someone's home is on fire. Dear God! I hope it's not ours" David slows down as he realizes we won't be able to drive down our street.

"There's Chelsea," I say. "I'll be right back." I jump out of the car to find out what's going on while David stares ahead, entranced.

A few moments later, I got back into the car.

"Well, what happened?" David says. "It looks like Frank's home."

"It is," I say. "Chelsea said she just pulled up a few minutes before we did. We should be able to get down the street shortly. She talked with an officer who said that no one has been injured and apparently Frank is said to be safe too. There aren't any details yet as to how the fire started, but it's just about under control. She says it wasn't a very big fire. But how can one tell by all that smoke, the two fire trucks, EMS, and multiple police cars?"

"Wow! It could've easily been our home," David says. "I'm so grateful we didn't have to come home to an incredible mess like this."

"Yes," I say as I grab David's hand, "me too. It makes me appreciate that I have someone to come home to. Poor Frank lives all alone."

"You're right. I don't often think about how others navigate living alone. We're so blessed. I love you."

"I love you too."

We lean in and kiss.

Chapter 33

Lisa

I had been milling around the house for a while after finishing my shift at the hospital. I was just going from room to room, tidying up and dusting a bit, when I looked out my front window and saw smoke coming from the rear of Frank's house. It didn't concern me at first; it wasn't very much smoke, so I figured he was burning something or starting up his grill.

By the time I'd finished my rounds and headed to the living room to sit and relax, I noticed the smoke was bigger and darker. I strained to look and see what was amiss, then decided to call 911 when Frank was nowhere in sight. I grabbed my cell phone and stood on the porch, talking to the 911 operator.

When she answered, I quickly said, "I think my neighbor's house is on fire." The operator asks me a series of questions which I answer quickly. "No. I don't think anyone is home. It looks like it's coming from the rear of the house. Should I go check?"

The operator tells me to steer clear and that the fire department is on the way. Just as I hang up, Rhonda walks up.

"Lisa? I was in my backyard checking on my garden when I smelled what I thought was smoke. I came to the front to see what was happening and saw smoke coming from Frank's house. I hollered his name as I tried to peek around the back. I don't think he's even home. What's happening?" There's a fire!

"I don't know. You may've heard me talking to emergency services. They're on the way. They said not to go towards the smoke. It could be dangerous."

No sooner than I finished my sentence, we both turned our heads as we heard the fire department approaching.

"Thank goodness they arrived so quickly. I don't have Frank's cellphone number, or I would call him. I don't want him to think I had something to do with this. I never have liked Frank, but I wouldn't dare want to see his house burn down."

Rhonda looked at me like she was struggling to believe me. "I only have his house number. He's not home, so that wouldn't be helpful. I saw his car going up the street about an hour ago."

We both stood on the curb now, watching as the firemen flew into action. To be truthful, seeing all these men in their gear, running here and there with the giant hose, made me feel some excitement. Who knew how sexy it would look to see men fighting a real fire? I fanned myself a bit.

"Are you okay?" Rhonda asks.

"Oh, yes, I'm fine. I just finished working out inside. I'm a little warm," I lie.

"Oh, do you need to sit down? You do look a little flushed."

"It's fine. I'll just head inside to get a little water; it looks like these good men have things under control. See ya, Rhonda."

"Bye."

I head back inside the house thinking that I feel a bit more than flushed. I have a mind to make a fresh batch of iced tea or something to seduce one of those fire men onto my porch and into my bed. I laugh at the thought while truly considering a cool glass of water. I feel a little more than hot and bothered, that's for sure.

Chapter 34

As I practically float outside the doors of the Department of Justice, I'm whistling. I cannot remember the last time I've felt this positive. It took some time, but I've convinced a friend to do some digging for me and he thinks he found a lead on Kaylee's whereabouts. The time spans seem to be lining up to the last time I saw her with whatever database he used. In all likelihood, he may have a ping to where she might've gone, more correctly, where her mother took her.

It seems he found flight details for three to St. Thomas that correspond with the dates I gave them. It will only take a matter of hours for them to cross check the photos of Kaylee and her mom I gave them. Although my name was put on my daughter's birth certificate, her mom used her last name for Kaylee. Thanks to servers or the cloud; whatever it's called, flight information can be stored for many years. My friend told me allowing Kaylee to be flown to the island wouldn't raise a red because, technically, it's a United States territory. So, it's not considered out of the country.

As much as I want to drive to a bar to have a drink to celebrate, I have to be coherent whenever the call comes in from the DOJ. So, I get in the car, turn the music up way too high, and start off towards home in the best mood I've been in for years.

A few minutes later, I'm pulling onto my street and immediately notice something going on. I turn the music off. There's a fire chief car and a fire truck at the curb of my house; as I drew closer to my home and saw a few neighbors on the sidewalk chatting in front of my house. The neighbors all at once turn and look at me with puzzled faces. That's when I noticed my front lawn was drenched.

My heart thumps as I put my car into park as close as I can to my house because my driveway is blocked. I take a deep breath and get out of my car.

"Hello, are you Mr. Frank Shefield?" a man says with the word "Fire Chief" on his shirt.

"Yes. I am. What's the situation here?"

"I'm sorry to tell you this, Mr. Shefield, but there's been a fire at your house. A neighbor called 911 earlier today to notify the department. When we got there, the fire appeared to have started in the rear of the house. Thankfully, the fire damage was contained in the rear of the home. My men are taking a closer look now; but the water damage seems to be also minimal. Presently, it looks as if one up-stairs room, the kitchen, and laundry room that holds the most damage."

I stand there speechless as I'm trying desper-ately to understand everything the chief is explain-ing.

I finally say thank you when I can enunciate a couple of words. Just then, a man with giant letters on his shirt boasting, "Fire Inspector," comes from the rear of my house. He's talking with the fire chief, but I can't hear anything as I know my neighbors are also talking and pointing. But all I hear is the dizzy-ing buzz from trying to process too much information all at once.

The next minute, Rhonda is at my side. "Frank? We're all here for you. We're so sorry this has happened to you."

"I need to sit," I say as I drop to the curb to take deep breaths and try to slow my heart. "Wow! This is a lot." I was just experiencing a tremendous high, and now I'm feeling an overwhelmingly low feeling.

"It's understandable, Frank, to be over-whelmed by what you just got home to," Rhonda says. As Rhonda reassured me everything would be okay, the fire chief approached.

"Mr. Sheffield? The cause of the fire is identi-fied as being from the presence of aluminum wiring coupled with the heat of the dryer in the laundry room. The heat of the dryer proved too much for the poor choice of the protection the wiring gives which has not been up to code for one of these specific reasons."

Rhonda and I look at each other. I have not installed any new wires since I bought this house. It was brand new when I bought it too.

"It might be a good idea to request the original drawings of the home to check and see if the whole house has been wired that way. If it was, that may mean the rest of these homes were, too." I couldn't believe what the fire chief just said, the whole community!

"Oh my God!" Rhonda says. The other neighbors in listening distance chime in as well.

"So, it's not my fault for leaving the dryer on while I was away? I've done it hundreds of times before."

"We certainly don't recommend that for obvious safety reasons, no matter how new a build. It was most like the result of the wiring getting hotter over time from use. It would've eventually caught on fire regardless of whether you were home or not. But again, do check the county records. They will have the original material list."

I stand and shake his hand. "Thank you. I will do that right away. Is it safe for me to go in?"

"Yes, albeit a bit wet and messy, but you can go in."

My good news is so far, at the back of my mind, I might as well have forgotten it as I began to walk around to the back of my home to assess the damage.

Chapter 35

Mike

I've never felt such panic as I did last week, hearing all those sirens just as I was pulling into my garage. I thought for sure the police were hot on my trail, about to arrest me for stealing from my job. I was so disheveled that I didn't even notice the smoke coming from Frank's house.

I'd finally caught my breath when I realized that the sirens were fire trucks. The first thought after that was that Lisa went and burned down Frank's house. Oh my God! What has she done? But, after hearing all the neighborhood chatter, it turns out there was an electrical problem that caused the fire, not Lisa.

And now, we've come to find out we're all in danger. The entire community was built using aluminum wiring throughout which is something contractors don't use anymore. The city strongly recommended that we all get our houses re-wired. I pick up the phone to call my sister. She answers on the first ring.

"Hello," she says.

"Hi Mary! I'm just checking to make sure your house isn't up in flames."

She huffs. "That's not funny, Mike. We're all in serious danger. I can't believe the whole community was built with this faulty wiring."

"I know," I say, "I was just joking. Lighten up."

"Well, I spoke with my insurance company a day ago; they called me back today and said they will not cover an entire re-wire. So, we will likely have to make a claim with the builders and have them do the work."

"I already knew that, Mary. My insurance told me that same thing three days ago."

"Oh!" Mary says. "I guess I'm a bit out of sorts with everything happening so fast."

"Just relax," I say, "everything will sort itself out. We'll be okay until things get sorted out."

"You're right, Mike. What else is going on?"

"Actually, not much of anything my way. Just the usual: work, play, rest, and work again. I told Mom about all the action last week. She told me she wanted to drive by to see the fire damage. But I told her not to bother because it was contained to the back of the house.

I'm just about to head over to the mall to meet her in half an hour. She needs a new pair of sunglasses, and they must be the Eddie Bauer brand."

I laugh and wish Mary good luck. "You know, Mary, there's no way it will take less than three hours at the mall. She will happen upon some other item she just didn't know the mall had and will insist on trying it on."

I know, Mike, but hopefully, some handsome man will notice how patient I am with her and will want to buy me lunch sometime." We both laugh.

"Alright, sis, I got to go, have fun."

"Talk to you soon. Bye."

As I hang up the phone, I hear a knock at my door. I put my phone on the counter to go see who it is. I look out the peephole to see a young lady I don't recognize.

I don't want nothing she's selling, I think as I open my front door. "Yes," I say.

"Hello," she says timidly. "I'm looking for Frank..."

Chapter 36

Kaylee

I hug Roy before I turn to go through the gate at the airport. I promise to call him if I need any-thing and let him know when my flight lands in Ohio. I can see now why my mom loved him so much. He was really helpful throughout all my questions and sometimes selfish words I spoke when I told him I was looking for Frank. Although he didn't know much about him, Columbus, Ohio, was a great place to start—even though thousands of people were there with the first name Frank.

I wish I had pestered my mother with more questions about him. Every time I asked, she said that Roy was my stand-in father. She was always so visibly annoyed and sometimes upset when I asked about my "real father," too. So, I eventually stopped asking.

I was surprised at how little Roy actually knew about the man he technically stole my mom from. But apparently, that's how my mom wanted it to be. Knowing that I'd been just a short flight away from my real dad all these years feels quite poetic. I'm still very nervous about whether he will want to see me at all.

Later, as the flight attendants walked up and down the aisle, I leaned back into my seat and took a deep breath. I don't think I've ever been anywhere without my mother. A tear slipped down my cheek unannounced. That happened sometime now since my mom passed. I just start crying from a simple thought or memory of her.

A few minutes later, the flight takes off. I pull my computer out when it's safe to do so and look at my Excel spreadsheet, filled with hundreds of people with the first name Frank. I've spent weeks crossing out all the names I eliminated from cold calls. I eventually narrowed the list down to less than a hundred "Franks" from the city I was born in. Roy found my birth certificate with Frank's first name but not his last name. But who knows if Frank still lives there?

I prioritized my list on how I would approach things once I landed. Then I decide to close my computer and take a quick nap. Before long, I'd awoke once the flight lands, and it was time to disembark the plane.

I text Roy that I'd landed safely, grab my bag, then caught an uber to get to the room I'd rented through Airbnb. Although I hadn't been outside St. Thomas for many years, I was familiar with the scenery as I rode to my destination. I can't really say I remember any of it, but it feels comfortable.

After arriving at home away from home, I start making phone calls immediately. Finding that some "Franks" had passed, moved, didn't have a daughter, no one answered, or numbers had been changed. I was getting more and more excited as my list grew smaller and smaller. I decided to call it a night, get some sleep, and start out again after breakfast.

Refreshed the next morning, I was in the shared kitchen explaining why I was here to my host. I wasn't old enough to rent a car although I was eighteen, but once I told my host my situation, she decided to lend me a car that used to belong to her husband. I thanked her profusely and went to get my door-to-door list so I could get started right away.

After knocking on several doors to discover none of the homes belonged to my Frank, I got back into the loaner car. I look at my watch and the sky and determined that I might have time for one or two more addresses before I'd need to grab some dinner and call it a night. I cross this last stop off and drove to the next one.

I was following Google maps to a well-kept neighborhood where all the homes looked pretty similar. The map took me to a house that looked like it was under construction by the looks of the men walking back and forth across the yard. So, I pull over and look around for a minute. The garage was up on the house directly across the street, so I decide to knock there instead.

My heart rate increases as I got up to the porch and knock on the door. A few seconds later a middle-aged man opens the door.

"Yes," he says.

"Hello," I say, "I'm looking for Frank. Google Maps led me to this neighborhood, but I'm unsure if it has the right house. Do you know him?" I glance back at the house under construction. "Or if he lives there?"

Chapter 37

Frank

I am completely exhausted as I sit in my living room, I returned a while ago after a very long morning negotiating with the builders. I can't be bothered with my normal curiosity from seeing the back of some lady on Mike's porch. Probably selling something I don't want to be bamboozled into buying like I normally do anyhow. I just want to sit on my couch with my eyes closed for a few minutes. My home is still under construction and would be for five or six more days from what the contractors have told me. Although I'm able to stay in my home during this period, it's quite noisy all the same.

Of course, I can't use the house's kitchen or other back areas. But I remain grateful that the water and fire damage were contained in such a small area. As I lean down to untie and take my gym shoes off, I have this weird feeling I can't explain. But I go into the dining room to open up my computer, the area I have been working in these past few days. It's a pretty safe spot in the house, even though it's noisy. There's no flying debris or drywall dust because of the tarp-like cover separating the living and dining rooms.

My front doorbell rings as I typed my password on my computer. I jump up, admittedly a little annoyed since I'd just sat down. Who could this be? The fire has been the talk of the neighborhood for days. I wish everyone would just get over it already. I swung the door open with a little more attitude than normal and gasp...

"Kaylee!"

I didn't even have to ask. I knew it was her before she said a word. All at once my body gave way to tears, joy, pain, and other emotions bottled up for years as I swung the screen door open and gathered her into my arms. I cannot believe I'm actually holding my sweet Kaylee again after all these years of dreaming of this moment. The world goes blank as I squeeze her tightly while crying the ugliest cry known to man. After a minute, I convince myself that this is real, to loosen my grip and let her breathe.

"Dad?" This beautiful girl looks me in the face with just as many tears as I do. "I was afraid you might not want to see me," she says.

"Kaylee! I've been searching for you for nearly eleven years."

We hug again. I touch her face, kiss her cheeks, and rub her arms. I can't believe this is real. I must be dreaming.

"Dad, I've been looking for you too. We have a lot of catching up to do. That's if you want to."

"Of course I want to," I say, "please come inside. It's a bit of a war zone right now. There was a fire that broke out recently in my laundry room. But there's time for all that later. I want to hear everything about you, Kaylee."

As we sit on the couch, I cannot bring myself to let go of her hand, in fear of losing her again. She doesn't seem to mind that I haven't let her go.

"Dad," Kaylee starts, "I had these vague memories of you for years. But with each passing year, your face became more and more blurred. I remember the feeling of being happy in your arms. When Mom passed a few months back, I knew I had to find you. I don't remember all of the details when we first left, but it was quick, like we were sneaking away. Mom was so happy and excited and that is how she stayed all the way up until her passing from a heart issue. She was so happy with Roy; he was just always there. She never talked about you, Frank, so it's taken me so long to find you."

"I'm so sorry about your mom, Kaylee."

The two of us sat and talked about our lives for hours. I couldn't take my eyes off Kaylee as she lit up about all her adventures in school, with friends, on the beach, and other details of her life in St.

Thomas. I was afraid that if I excused myself to the restroom, I would come back to an empty room. So, I didn't go.

After a while, I ask, "Are you hungry? I know a great place about fifteen minutes away that we could go to. Her smile almost melted me.

"Yes, I am getting hungry."

"Well, let me go upstairs to change my shirt and go to the restroom. There's a restroom in the hallway if you need to go."

"Okay," she says.

"Here, I'll show you, follow me." We take the stairs into the short hallway and I pat the doorframe of the bathroom just to my left. "I'll be right back; I'm going to go into my room real quick. Feel free to look around."

I move like the speed of lightning to hurry back out to Kaylee. Before I leave my bedroom, I grab the photo to show her what I've kept with me all these years. I finally reached the bottom of the stairs and watched my daughter meandering around my living room. My eyes go blurry while my heart is over-whelmed with disbelief by this most sought-after prayer that has finally been answered.

Chapter 38

Rhonda

Well, what can I say? What a difference a day makes. That's what they say and now I understand why. The neighborhood has finally calmed down after all the action we've had around here last year. All the construction with our homes getting completely rewired took some time. Now, we can all claim an upgrade. Mary has moved out of the neighborhood and so has Lisa. Who would've guessed? What a huge shift the neighborhood has taken.

Not only that, but ever since I came clean to Frank about the HOA violations I've been pointing out for years, I have more time on my hands not doing that anymore. I used to wonder about him and now the two of us are really good friends. It's amazing how we can connect as humans through a few candid conversations.

Now that I'm not secretly being a busybody, I've been spending more time in my garden and with my children. I'm excited about finally expecting my first grandchild in a few months. I have a pretty satisfying life between visiting life-long friends, my garden, my part-time job, and the other day-to-day. I didn't see it before, but having a little empathy as well as imagining walking a mile in someone else's shoes goes a long way. I used to mostly stay to myself, but now I'm pretty social with my other neighbors.

There's not a week that goes by Frank and I don't talk, even with Kaylee back in his life. I'm thrilled for him; he is the happiest I've ever seen him. I no longer see pain in his eyes, just pride and joy these days. I'm so glad we've managed to stay friends.

I'm pretty much the produce lady in the neighborhood now. Frank told everyone last year about our bounty. I don't mind, though. Frank and a few other neighbors have started a small garden of their own this year. Some just start off with one vegetable to see how easy it is.

I still don't know who put that strange sign in Frank's yard last year. Although I still imagine it was Lisa. Since she's no longer here, there's been no more funny business going on around here. I guess the saying, "One bad apple spoils the whole bunch," carries some truth to it. I don't plan on moving anywhere else. I love my home and its proximity to my children, friends, and job. Also, who knows if Mr. Wonderful might be just a house or two away?

Chapter 39

Patricia

I never have agreed with people who believed ignorance is bliss. I have always believed that the more I know, the better equipped I am to decide on what's going to come next. Living in this neighborhood has taught me some very valuable lessons.

One is that it's good to be able to rely on one another. David and I were operating in a more independent way even though we were married. We'd been so efficiently moving from one level to the next at work, we forgot we were a single unit. His slip up brought us back to depending on each other in ways that have strengthened our communication, together time, and spiritual connection as well.

It was hard to swallow the lesson of not being above reproach. I thought I had my life so put together before my husband almost made an indiscretion. I walked around with my nose pointed up without even realizing it. I found out trouble can easily knock on my door just as easily as anyone else's. I barely dodged some serious heartache, and today, I'm more grateful than ever that we were able to get through the hard times together.

Now that I don't appear so arrogant, I'm not the last one to hear the scoop anymore. It may also have something to do with the days following the accident. All the neighbors were so comforting, we've become more of a tribe than ever; always looking out for one another.

We've both reduced our hours at work to forty per week relatively consistently now. So, we now have plenty of time to connect daily to investigate each other's ever-changing love languages. I find solace in that we didn't need to continue to make a lot of money because this neighborhood allows us to live within our means.

There's no contention to be heard of between Frank and the others from the neighborhood anymore. I don't think he would have time to talk about who has it out for him now that his daughter is living with him. Never mind the fact that I've lived here ten years and didn't even know Frank had a daughter.

David and I walk together around the neighborhood at least three or four days per week. Sometimes, we even run. I love him so much more than ever. Understanding that life can change in an instant has really changed me. I care about people in a way that I have never had before. David and I have rekindled our flame, and life is good. Now, my last order of business is to make sure he never finds out about my one-night stand.

Chapter 40

Mary

I look over the brim of my sunglasses at a handsome guy jogging down the beach. I'm almost tempted to get up and go running after him. For what, I don't know. Maybe I'll tell him he dropped something and when he asks, what? I can just say me.

Mom brought me back from my salacious trance when I heard, "Honey, you want another drink?"

"No, Mom, I'm fine. But have another if you'd like."

"Okay, suit yourself," she says. As I watch my mom head back to the beach bar, I have to pinch myself again. I still couldn't believe she talked me into moving to Florida with her. She raved and raved about this beautiful condo she saw near the beach, preaching how wonderful it would be to walk to the beach every day. And would you guess she was right? I love it here.

It was time for a change after all the drama from the neighborhood back in Ohio. After the contractors finished rewiring my home, I put it on the market for sale. Just as I thought, it sold quickly, in less than a month. I was able to close it on the contingency of getting a condo in Florida. I purchased one in the same community where Mom lives. It all worked out smoothly.

I will never have to bake another pie again. Or at least for any neighbors, they have all sorts of bakeries and specialty shops nearby. Boy, was I getting tired of being nice all the time. Everyone kept calling me the nicest or sweetest person ever, and before long, I was pretending to be just that. I wish I could've got one more prank in on Frank before I moved. I can't believe he turned me down all those years ago when I came on to him. Rejection doesn't feel good at all.

I mean I was single. He was single, at least, I thought he was. He was running around the neighborhood one day a year or two after the core group was settled. I'd invited him inside and he seemed to be into me, so I gave it a go. But I must've got my signals all wrong. It was so embarrassing! Now, looking back, I should've just swallowed my pride instead of holding a grudge all those years. I didn't notice how holding onto spite affected me until I got here to Florida and let it all go. I haven't felt so light in a while and I'm loving it.

To my knowledge, nobody figured out that it was me who put that sign in his yard. I guess I didn't have to hold a grudge for so long, but he really hurt my feelings. Anyway, I heard from Mike that he has a daughter and everything now. I often forget that I ever met the guy. That is until Mike calls and fills me in on all the things going on in the neighborhood. Other than sharing my pastries with Mom, I'll have to keep my pies and *goodies* to myself for a while.

Chapter 41

Chelsea

School is finally out for the summer again. It's hard to believe this will be Ariel and I's second summer here in our new home. Maybe it's not so new anymore, but it still feels that way. We both really love it here. Although there have been a few eventful things previously in the neighborhood, things have quieted down a whole lot.

Frank hasn't come around nearly as much since his daughter has moved in with him. It was kind of weird for me at first meeting her when he introduced us. Oddly, she resembles me; not just in looks but mannerisms too. Although she's a few years younger than me, she seems like a really nice girl. For some reason, Frank seems a little less strange now that she's around. It's funny how people can change you that way.

I'm so proud of Ariel, she did great this school year, earning all A's and B's. At fourteen years old, she still loves her puzzles and board games. These days she started dancing and to my surprise, she's pretty good at it. Of all things, ballroom is the style she took to. I don't mind, though, because she gets to be dressed up in the most beautiful dresses. It's a

little expensive but she loves it, and I'll always appreciate that at least she's not twerking.

I do miss Mary's visits and her delicious pies.
She calls every few months to tell me about this guy
and that one she's met or gone on a date with. She
sounds really happy with her move to Florida. There
still was just something that kept nagging me about
her, but I guess I'll never know what it was. But
there is something I've been hiding from her. Mike
and I have been hooking up for a few months now. I
saw him one night when I was out, and the rest is,
well...great. Neither of us craves anything serious,
but we like each other's company well enough to
keep things going. I have to admit, that surprised
me.

All in all, this neighborhood has been more
than I bargained for in a good way. I see myself living here until at least Ariel graduates from high
school. Who knows where life will take me after
that? I'm open to whatever may come my way. Ariel
talks about my preserved seeds, dehydrated foods,
and other prepping now, but she'll appreciate me if
we have another government shutdown or serious
food shortage. Lord knows I have enough for the
whole neighborhood!

Chapter 42

Mike

This neighborhood is going to lack a lot of action now that my sister and Lisa have both moved away. Now I won't have any crazy stories about Lisa anymore, unless she harasses Frank from afar. But there's probably not a chance of that because everyone got all motherly ever since we found out Frank had a daughter. I know I was shocked. Lisa told me before packing up that she should kill all Franks' plants in the front yard. But they're still thriving, so I guess she chickened out.

My job has been keeping me busy anyway. It turns out I quit skimming from the company at just the right time. A few months later, I got a promotion. Imagine that! A raise, too. I'm counting my lucky stars every day now. I've been arriving ten minutes early and leaving five minutes late just to express showmanship.

Mary and Mom love it in Florida, I hear from them both all the time. They want me to come down and visit soon. I told them about my promotion and that I'd have to hold off for a few months and then take a long weekend. But I'm glad they're enjoying themselves. I think the two of them are the sweetest and most deserving people. Although, I will miss Mary's pies. I'll always have a place to stay in sunny Florida.

All that wondering I did about Chelsea when she first moved to the neighborhood was settled one night when we ran into each other in a bar. I had no idea she would frequent the same sort of place as I would. It turned out, it was both of our first times at the bar. Because we knew each other, we struck up a conversation had more than a few drinks, then one thing led to another. I'll be a gentleman and say that we did not go home right away that night. Being with Chelsea gives me a kind of clarity I didn't know I needed. She doesn't want Ariel to know about us yet, so I agreed to keep things quiet for now, which is perfect for me. I don't feel the need to speed towards any public declarations.

My past is proof that I do most things behind closed doors. In fact, Mom and Mary always believed Dad drank himself to death. Well, that's partially true. I may've had sped the process up a little. He was killing himself anyway and killing Mom's spirit every day of his miserable life. Let's just say Lisa isn't the only one who knows how to slip something into someone's drink. I'll never repeat this out loud. But I'll never regret seeing the relief on Mom's face once he was finally gone, not for a single second.

Chapter 43

Lisa

I've come a long way from past traumas, torturing animals, and pestering Frank. When I first got to the neighborhood, I was an emotional reck from not being able to trust people, especially men. Over time, I became less disturbed and more interested in how others responded to less-than-ideal circumstances.

As an adult, I was able to direct my strange curiosities into the operating room. Speaking of the hospital, the good doctor and I never had a tryst or anything but turns out I did find out enough about him to know his wife was indeed very good to him. The more we talked about ourselves to each other, the more our friendship developed. As a matter of fact, he introduced me to a cousin of his that he thought I would hit it off with and it turned out we did. That is the reason I moved out of the neighborhood.

The doctor's cousin was visiting him from North Carolina at the time we met. I found out he worked as a pediatrician. Although he was only in town for the weekend, we managed to schedule a date each day he was here. Our chemistry was like magic. We really hit it off. After conversing and meeting for a couple of months, he asked me to move to North Carolina so that we could start a serious relationship. Of course, I said yes right away. I got a good price for my home, as I knew I would and bought a nice-sized condo in North Carolina just a few miles away from his.

Since I can no longer badger Frank anymore, I find I don't miss his reactions. They were priceless entertainment, I have to say. I channel all my energy these days into my new man as well as the interns coming to the hospital I now work for in North Carolina. I still get a thrill out of seeing the squeamish ones faint or get sick from the sight of blood. Overall, this new chapter of my life has been quite a satisfying thrill.

At times, I miss the comradery my previous co-workers and I had, but I still occasionally hear from my closest ones. They call and fill me in on their bar adventures. I hear about the good doctor from my boyfriend from time to time and am happy that he's doing well. One place I don't hear about is the old neighborhood because not too many were fond of me. That helped me realize that I had room to grow as a person. So, I'm being more of an approachable neighbor this time around, thanks to my boyfriend bringing the softer, more trusting side of me out.

But I could not begin the new me without one more devious act before I left the neighborhood. Frank will have found the surprise I left by now. I ordered a huge blowup balloon to be delivered and put in his front yard. I left explicit directions for the eight-foot blowup to be delivered early in the morning and left without ringing the doorbell. I, of course, had to pay extra for this prank with the company I used to stay anonymous. But man do I hope it was worth it. I only wish I was around to see his reaction.

Charity Pleasant

Chapter 44

Frank

Of all the things I have to be grateful for this past year, I'm still ecstatic that Kaylee is finally back in my life. It has been a long, long, time coming and took a lot of prayer, searching, and believing from me. And to think that it was her who found me and not the other way around. I'm over the moon that she decided to stay with me for a while so that we can reacquaint ourselves with each other. For her, the timing couldn't be more perfect after finishing high school because she wants to take a gap year to figure out college and her next steps in life anyway.

Of course, I told her not to worry about a thing as I would be there for any advice that she needed. I'm secretly hoping it will take her the longest time ever to figure things out, so I can have her here with me the longest time possible.

She's livened up things around here, adding some decorative touches to the house here and there. I made sure to tell her to do whatever will make the place feel most like home. For all I care, she could paint the entire house pink and I'd still be smiling like a Cheshire cat. I try not to smother her daily from simply wanting to make up for lost time. Although, I don't think she minds that much.

There's still plenty of work for me to do around the neighborhood with acclimating the new buyers and all. Along with my full-time job, with Kaylee, plus Rhonda, who has become a constant friend, my life feels pretty full. One day, I heard Kaylee yelling from downstairs for me to come quickly. I thought there was something terribly wrong. But when I made it to the bottom of the stairs, she was doubled over with laughter from her spot at the front door.

Upon looking through the open front door where she was pointing, because she literally couldn't get the words out, I saw a huge blow-up of male genitals in our front yard. I turned red with embarrassment but couldn't help but laugh, too. Her laughter was contagious.

"I know Lisa had something to do with it," I finally said after catching my breath. She just had to go off with a bang.

"Who's Lisa?" Kaylee asked.

"That's a long story."

It appeared there was a note with the monstrosity, too. She handed the note to me. It read: "Dear Frank, I hope you enjoy having a big.... For a while. XOXO." I have to admit that I'd never seen anything like this before. If this had occurred a while ago, I would've been out of my mind for a while. But I was able to just turn around, go into the kitchen, grab a steak knife so that I could go to the porch and burst the ridiculous inflatable. As we watched it deflate, we held onto each other for support, laughing so hard at the irony of what I just did.

Chapter 45

Kaylee

My life felt like it finally came full circle. On one hand, I have lived a life so uniquely spectacular in St. Thomas. The opportunities I've had to experience life to the fullest without any limitations are hard sought after. I always knew that my mother and Roy loved me because it was evident in how they cared for me. But on the other hand, there had always felt like a small part that was missing, and that part was my biological father.

Our reunion was better than I could've imagined because I'd always worried that there was a possibility he didn't want to know me. I've seen some movies that turned out exactly like that, and I knew it could be a worst-case scenario for me. But the fact that my father had never stopped looking for me proved that he loved me and never stopped doing so.

We spent so many days and nights just talking about our lives and dreams. My dad sticks a little close to me sometimes, wanting to include himself in any outing I venture out on. But I don't mind so much. I told him all about Roy one evening several months ago, and to my surprise, he said he sounded like a great guy. That was a weird response, know-ing that Roy went along with my mother in basically removing me from my dad's life. But that just showed how great he is on the inside.

I wasn't surprised by the few questions he had about my mom, after all, she used to be his girl-friend. I showed him a few pictures of her from my phone that showed how happy she'd been over the years and that was that.

It's amazing how fast a whole year can fly by. I've met so many of Frank's neighbors, who've made me feel a part of the neighborhood. But it's coming up in time for me to decide where I will apply to col-lege and how I will bridge my life in St. Thomas to Ohio. I had a few friends who were finishing their first-year stateside. They'd been giving me some ad-vice, too.

Frank told me that Ohio State was a great school, and I knew that he'd love for me to be nearby. As much as I was fond of Roy and appreciated all he had done for me over the years, being here with Frank feels more like home. I plan to apply for OSU and see if I get in this fall.

I can definitely make arrangements to fly to St. Thomas during my breaks and summers. And if Roy's willing to have me, I have no doubt he will. Who knows? Maybe one day, I'll write a book about all this.

After all, every neighborhood has its secrets and this one sure gave me plenty to tell.

The End

Resource Page

Start a business

1. https://www.sba.gov
2. https://www.ohiosos.gov/businesses/information-on-starting-and-maintaining-a-business/starting-a-business/

Write a book (Available at some local public libraries)

The Nonfiction Book Publishing Plan: The professional guide to profitable self-publishing. Stephanie Chandler and Karl W. Palachuk 2018

How to self-Publish for under $100: The step-by-step handbook to publish your book without breaking the bank. Cinquanta Cox-Smith 2017

Financial Help

(Book, Audiobook, or CD) David Bach: Debt Free for Life

Dave Ramsey: Financial Peace

Author Contacts:

Pleasantinvestments123@gmail.com

YouTube: Pleasant Investments

Website: Pleasantinvestments.com

www.ingramcontent.com/pod-product-compliance
Lightning Source LLC
Chambersburg PA
CBHW030429120726
47903CB00003B/879